JIA and the NIAN MONSTER

A TALE OF
ANCIENT CHINA

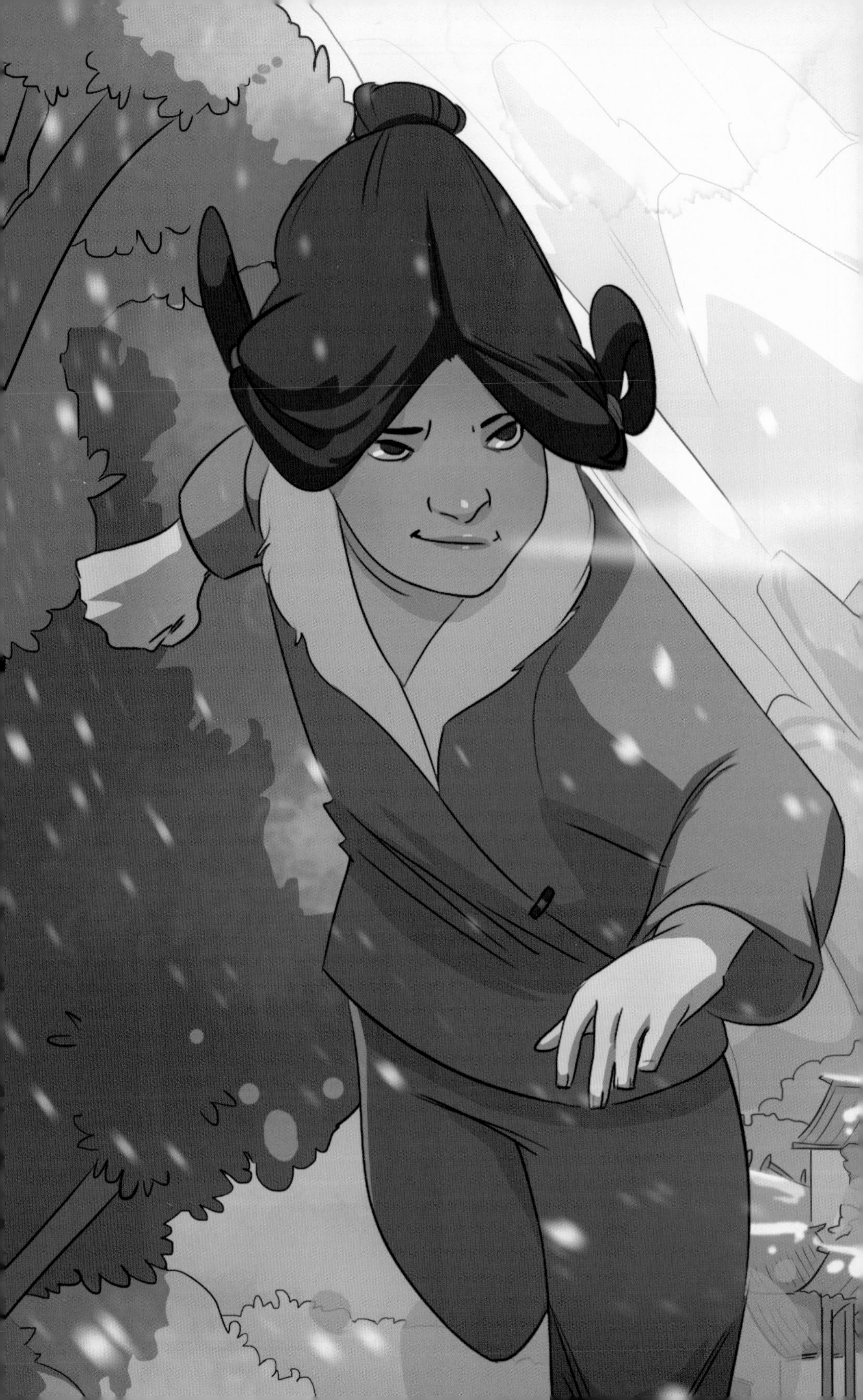

JIA and the NIAN MONSTER

SCRIPT BY
MIKE RICHARDSON

ART BY
MEGAN HUANG

❖

LETTERING BY
RICHARD STARKINGS
AND COMICRAFT'S
JIMMY BETANCOURT

COVER ART BY
MEGAN HUANG

DARK HORSE BOOKS

PRESIDENT & PUBLISHER
MIKE RICHARDSON

EDITOR
RANDY STRADLEY

ASSISTANT EDITOR
JUDY KHUU

DESIGNER
PATRICK SATTERFIELD

DIGITAL ART TECHNICIAN
ANN GRAY

JIA AND THE NIAN MONSTER

Jia and the Nian Monster is an original graphic novel.

Published by DARK HORSE BOOKS
A division of Dark Horse Comics LLC ❖ 10956 SE Main Street, Milwaukie, OR 97222

DarkHorse.com

To find a comics shop in your area, visit comicshoplocator.com

Library of Congress Cataloging-in-Publication Data

Names: Richardson, Mike, 1950- author. | Huang, Megan, illustrator.
Title: Jia and the Nian Monster / Mike Richardson, Megan Huang.
Description: Milwaukie, OR : Dark Horse Books, 2020. | Audience: Ages 10+ |
    Summary: "Each new year is marked by a monster's attack on their
    mountain village. This year, young Jia and her friend Deshi have decided
    to fight back. For Deshi, it is the grand adventure he has always
    dreamed of. For Jia, it is revenge for the loss of her mother-who was
    taken by the monster five years before."-- Provided by publisher.
Identifiers: LCCN 2019041182 | ISBN 9781506714967 (trade paperback)
Subjects: LCSH: Graphic novels. | CYAC: Graphic novels. |
    Monsters--Fiction. | Revenge--Fiction. | Adventure and
    adventurers--Fiction.
Classification: LCC PZ7.7.R53 Ji 2020 | DDC 741.5/973--dc23
LC record available at https://lccn.loc.gov/2019041182

First edition: March 2020
ISBN 978-1-50671-496-7

1 3 5 7 9 10 8 6 4 2
Printed in China

JIA and the Nian Monster

Prologue: The Legend

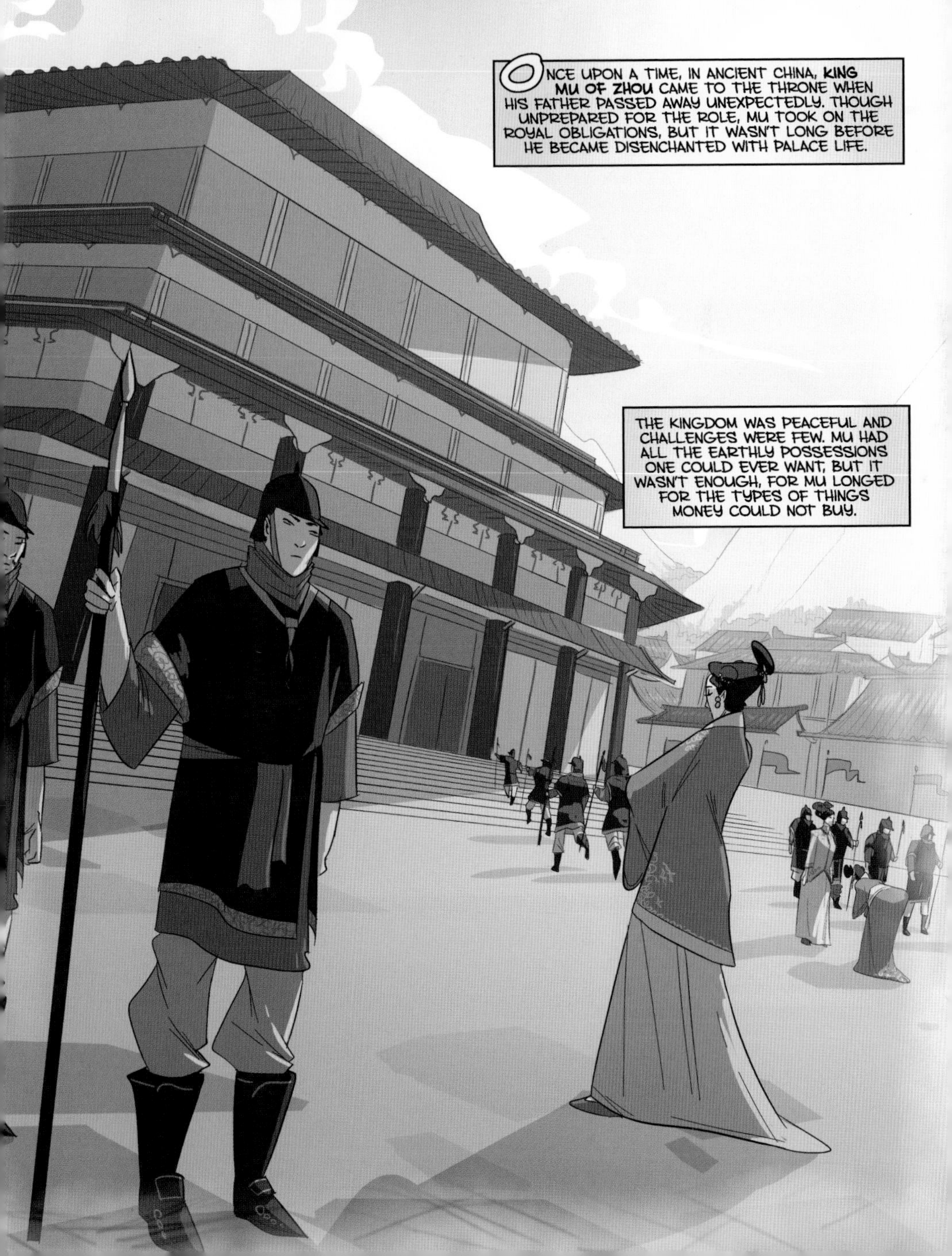
ONCE UPON A TIME, IN ANCIENT CHINA, KING MU OF ZHOU CAME TO THE THRONE WHEN HIS FATHER PASSED AWAY UNEXPECTEDLY. THOUGH UNPREPARED FOR THE ROLE, MU TOOK ON THE ROYAL OBLIGATIONS, BUT IT WASN'T LONG BEFORE HE BECAME DISENCHANTED WITH PALACE LIFE.
THE KINGDOM WAS PEACEFUL AND CHALLENGES WERE FEW. MU HAD ALL THE EARTHLY POSSESSIONS ONE COULD EVER WANT, BUT IT WASN'T ENOUGH, FOR MU LONGED FOR THE TYPES OF THINGS MONEY COULD NOT BUY.

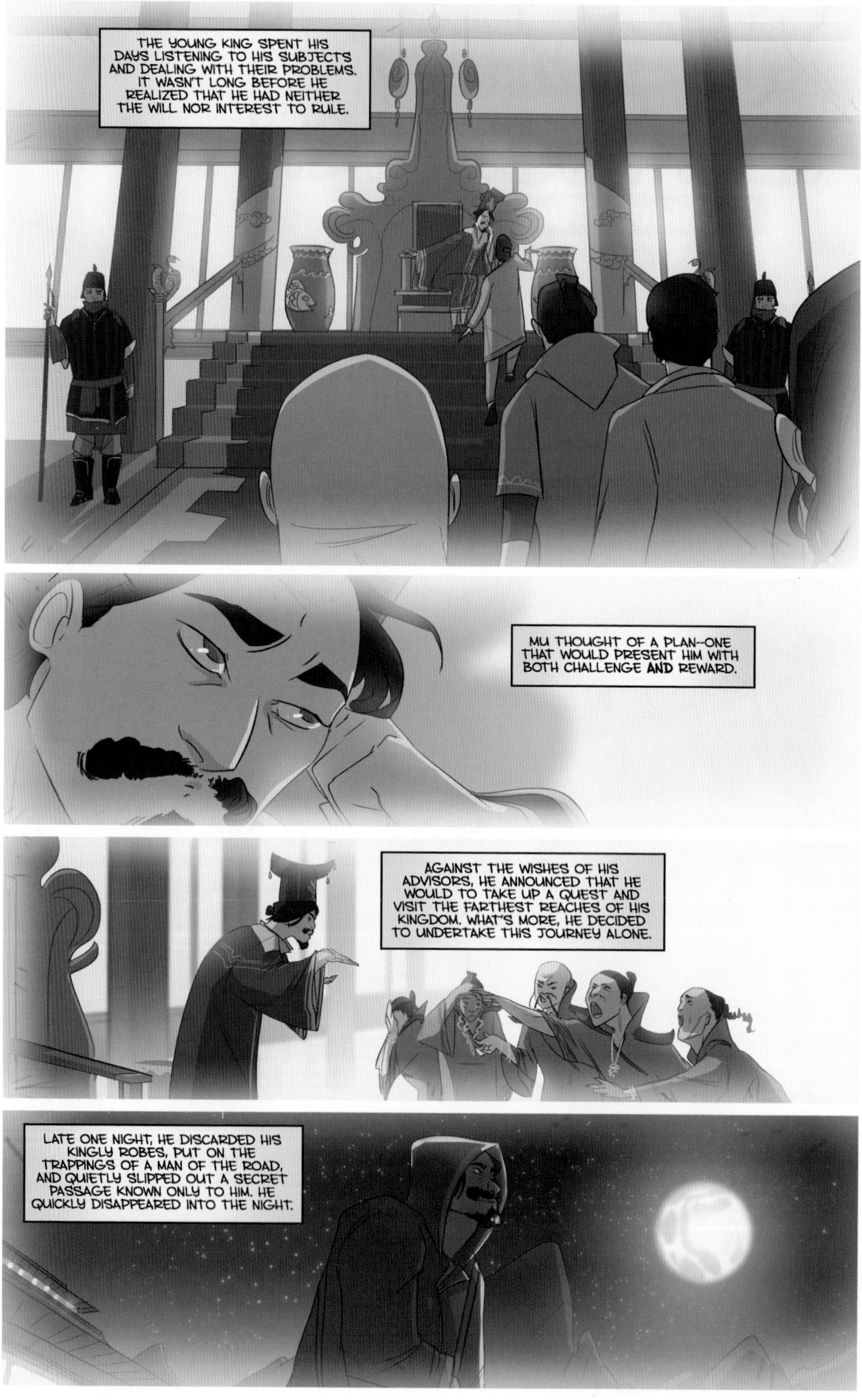
THE YOUNG KING SPENT HIS DAYS LISTENING TO HIS SUBJECTS AND DEALING WITH THEIR PROBLEMS. IT WASN'T LONG BEFORE HE REALIZED THAT HE HAD NEITHER THE WILL NOR INTEREST TO RULE.
MU THOUGHT OF A PLAN--ONE THAT WOULD PRESENT HIM WITH BOTH CHALLENGE **AND** REWARD.
AGAINST THE WISHES OF HIS ADVISORS, HE ANNOUNCED THAT HE WOULD TO TAKE UP A QUEST AND VISIT THE FARTHEST REACHES OF HIS KINGDOM. WHAT'S MORE, HE DECIDED TO UNDERTAKE THIS JOURNEY ALONE.
LATE ONE NIGHT, HE DISCARDED HIS KINGLY ROBES, PUT ON THE TRAPPINGS OF A MAN OF THE ROAD, AND QUIETLY SLIPPED OUT A SECRET PASSAGE KNOWN ONLY TO HIM. HE QUICKLY DISAPPEARED INTO THE NIGHT.

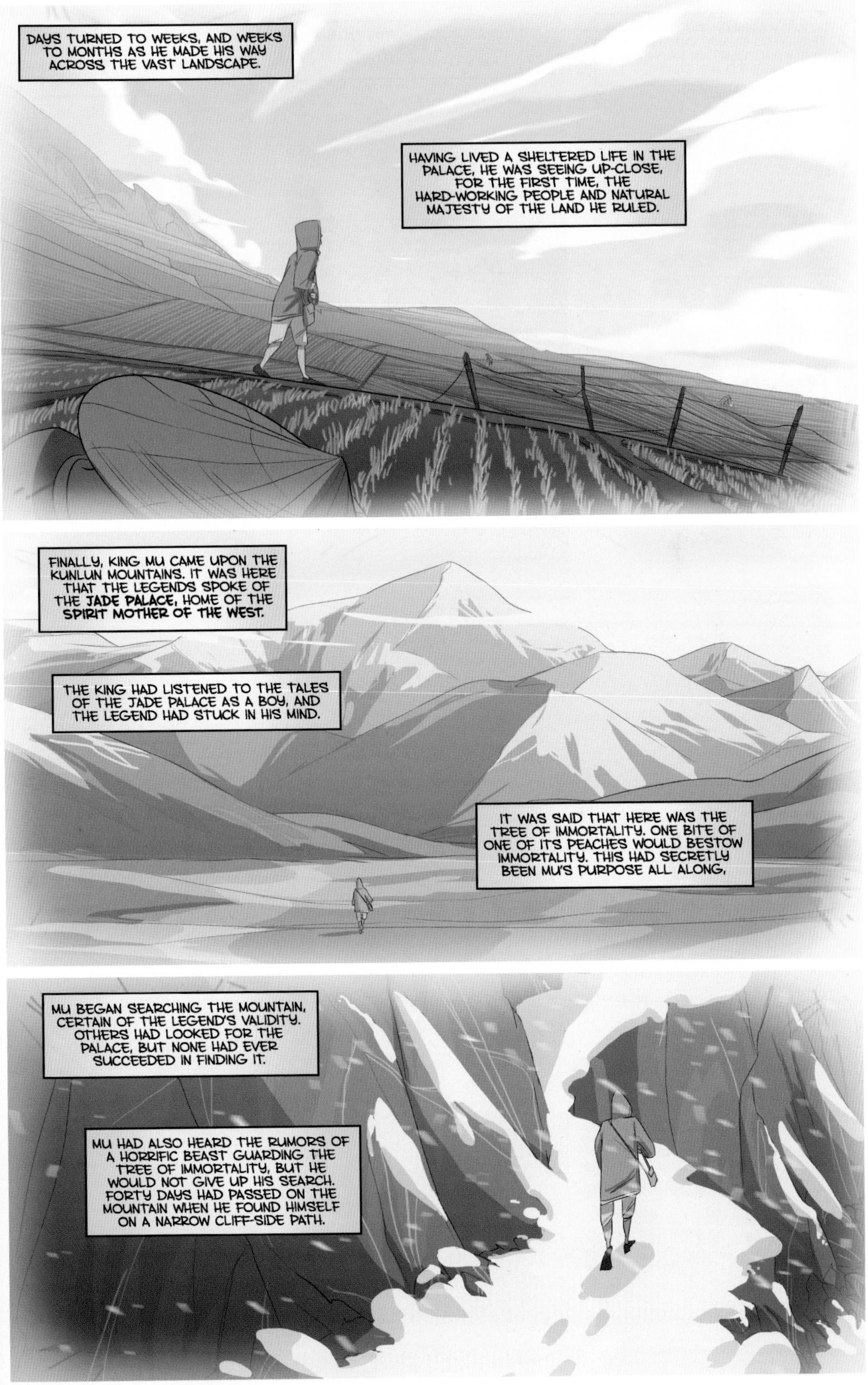
DAYS TURNED TO WEEKS, AND WEEKS TO MONTHS AS HE MADE HIS WAY ACROSS THE VAST LANDSCAPE.
HAVING LIVED A SHELTERED LIFE IN THE PALACE, HE WAS SEEING UP-CLOSE, FOR THE FIRST TIME, THE HARD-WORKING PEOPLE AND NATURAL MAJESTY OF THE LAND HE RULED.
FINALLY, KING MU CAME UPON THE KUNLUN MOUNTAINS. IT WAS HERE THAT THE LEGENDS SPOKE OF THE **JADE PALACE**, HOME OF THE **SPIRIT MOTHER OF THE WEST.**
THE KING HAD LISTENED TO THE TALES OF THE JADE PALACE AS A BOY, AND THE LEGEND HAD STUCK IN HIS MIND.
IT WAS SAID THAT HERE WAS THE TREE OF IMMORTALITY. ONE BITE OF ONE OF ITS PEACHES WOULD BESTOW IMMORTALITY. THIS HAD SECRETLY BEEN MU'S PURPOSE ALL ALONG.
MU BEGAN SEARCHING THE MOUNTAIN, CERTAIN OF THE LEGEND'S VALIDITY. OTHERS HAD LOOKED FOR THE PALACE, BUT NONE HAD EVER SUCCEEDED IN FINDING IT.
MU HAD ALSO HEARD THE RUMORS OF A HORRIFIC BEAST GUARDING THE TREE OF IMMORTALITY, BUT HE WOULD NOT GIVE UP HIS SEARCH. FORTY DAYS HAD PASSED ON THE MOUNTAIN WHEN HE FOUND HIMSELF ON A NARROW CLIFF-SIDE PATH.

WITHOUT WARNING, THE MOUNTAIN BEGAN TO SHAKE VIOLENTLY AND MU WAS CERTAIN HE WOULD PLUNGE TO HIS DEATH.

MIRACULOUSLY, THE QUAKE OPENED A FISSURE IN THE FACE OF THE MOUNTAIN...

...ALLOWING MU TO ESCAPE THE CRUMBLING LEDGE.

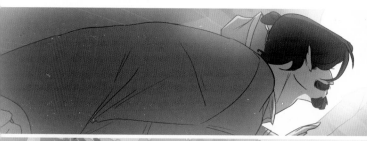

THE YOUNG KING MADE HIS WAY THROUGH THE NARROW PASSAGEWAY IN THE ROCK...

...AND WAS MET BY A WONDROUS SIGHT--A LUSH GARDEN. AND, TOWERING HIGH ABOVE, THE **JADE PALACE** OF LEGEND.

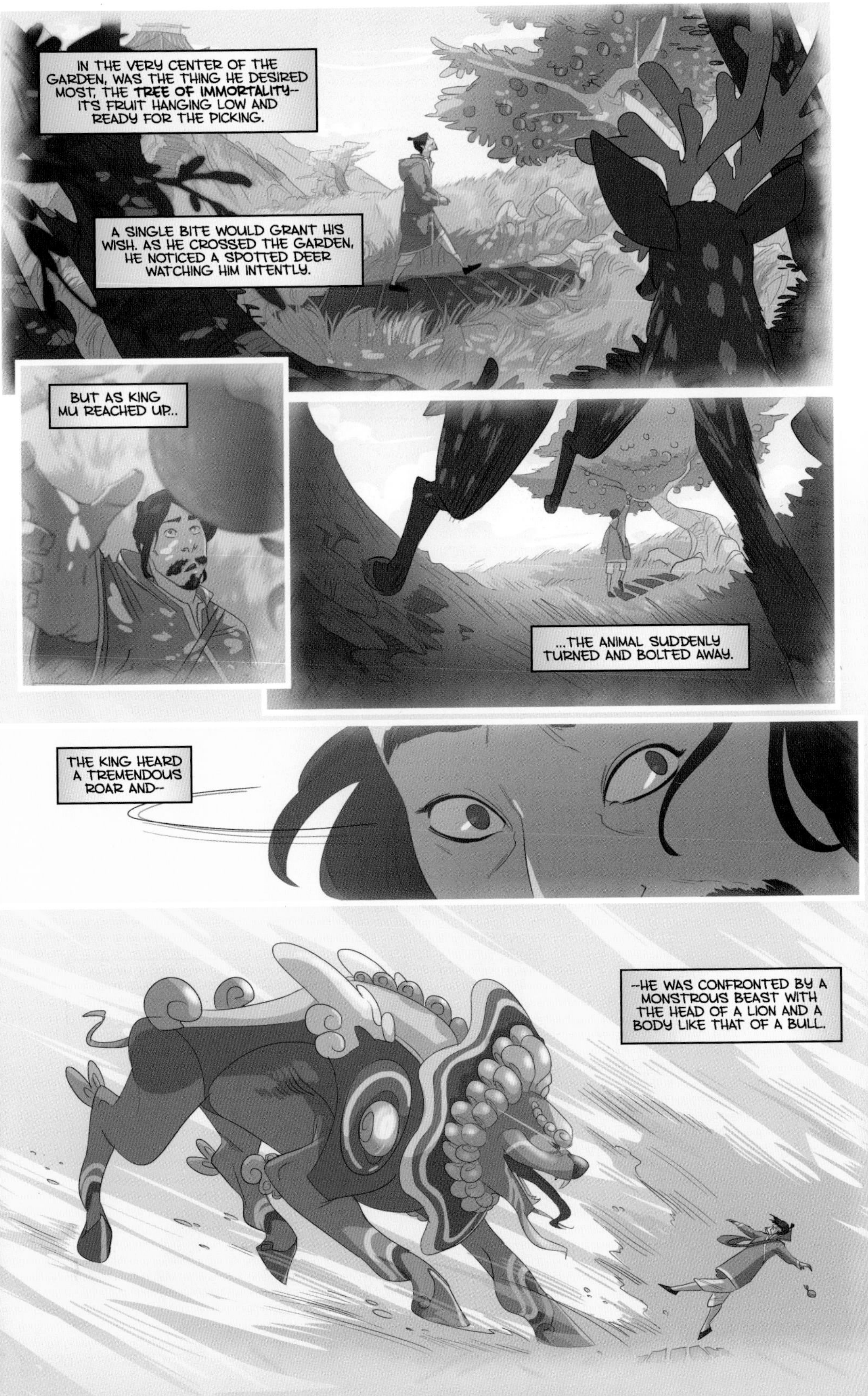
IN THE VERY CENTER OF THE GARDEN, WAS THE THING HE DESIRED MOST, THE **TREE OF IMMORTALITY**-- ITS FRUIT HANGING LOW AND READY FOR THE PICKING.
A SINGLE BITE WOULD GRANT HIS WISH. AS HE CROSSED THE GARDEN, HE NOTICED A SPOTTED DEER WATCHING HIM INTENTLY.
BUT AS KING MU REACHED UP...
...THE ANIMAL SUDDENLY TURNED AND BOLTED AWAY.
THE KING HEARD A TREMENDOUS ROAR AND--
--HE WAS CONFRONTED BY A MONSTROUS BEAST WITH THE HEAD OF A LION AND A BODY LIKE THAT OF A BULL.

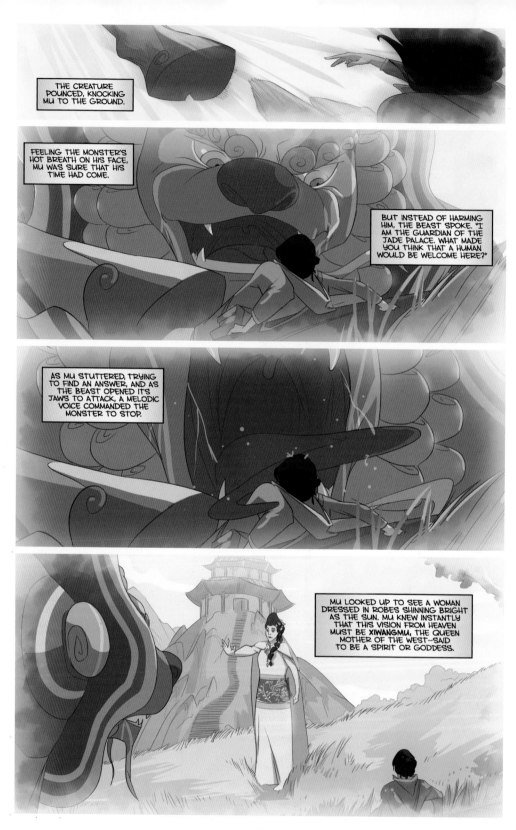

THE CREATURE POUNCED, KNOCKING MU TO THE GROUND.

FEELING THE MONSTER'S HOT BREATH ON HIS FACE, MU WAS SURE THAT HIS TIME HAD COME.

BUT INSTEAD OF HARMING HIM, THE BEAST SPOKE. "I AM THE GUARDIAN OF THE JADE PALACE. WHAT MADE YOU THINK THAT A HUMAN WOULD BE WELCOME HERE?"

AS MU STUTTERED, TRYING TO FIND AN ANSWER, AND AS THE BEAST OPENED ITS JAWS TO ATTACK, A MELODIC VOICE COMMANDED THE MONSTER TO STOP.

MU LOOKED UP TO SEE A WOMAN DRESSED IN ROBES SHINNING BRIGHT AS THE SUN. MU KNEW INSTANTLY THAT THIS VISION FROM HEAVEN MUST BE XIWANGMU, THE QUEEN MOTHER OF THE WEST--SAID TO BE A SPIRIT OR GODDESS.

10

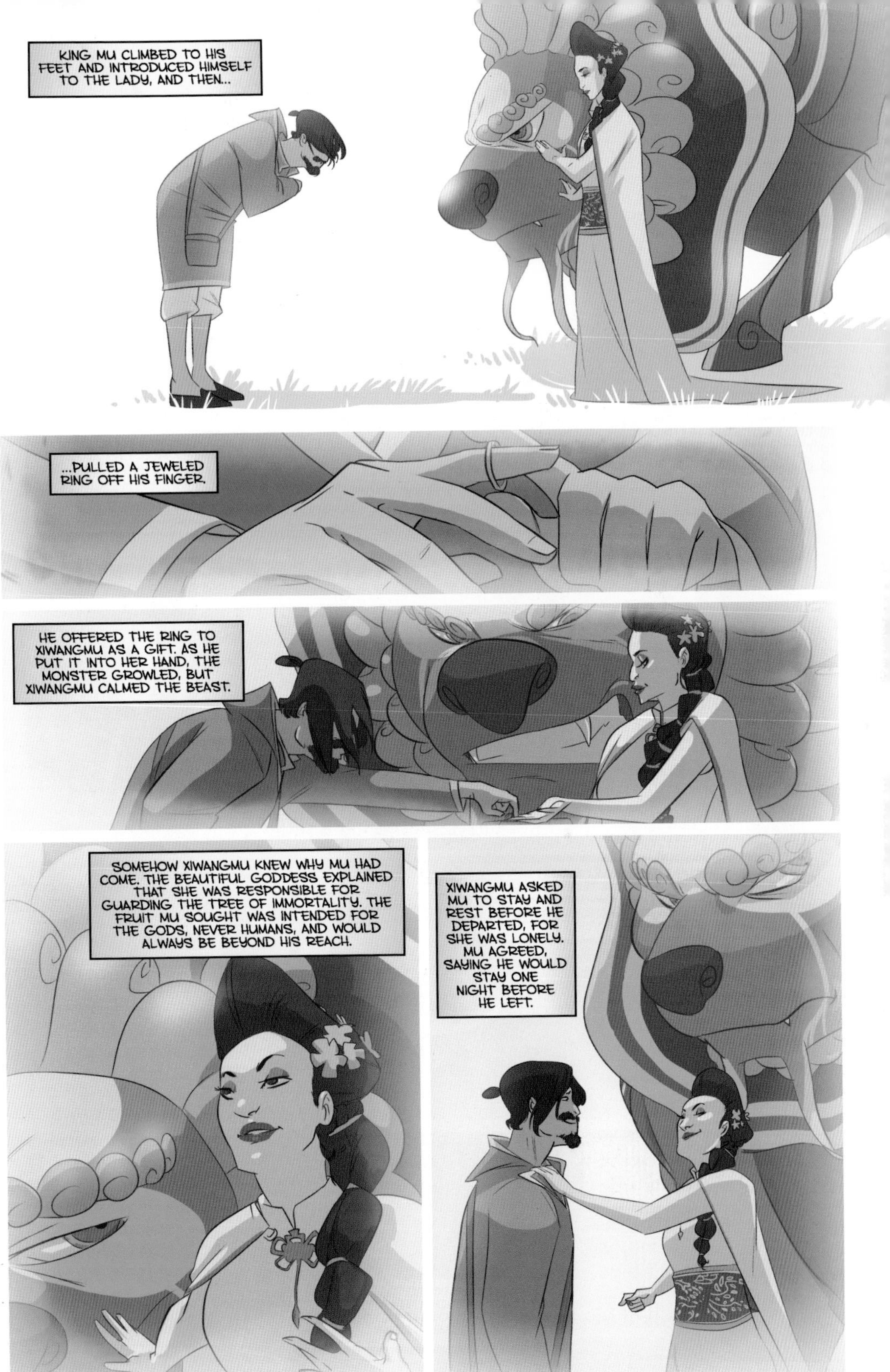
KING MU CLIMBED TO HIS FEET AND INTRODUCED HIMSELF TO THE LADY, AND THEN...
...PULLED A JEWELED RING OFF HIS FINGER.
HE OFFERED THE RING TO XIWANGMU AS A GIFT. AS HE PUT IT INTO HER HAND, THE MONSTER GROWLED, BUT XIWANGMU CALMED THE BEAST.
SOMEHOW XIWANGMU KNEW WHY MU HAD COME. THE BEAUTIFUL GODDESS EXPLAINED THAT SHE WAS RESPONSIBLE FOR GUARDING THE TREE OF IMMORTALITY. THE FRUIT MU SOUGHT WAS INTENDED FOR THE GODS, NEVER HUMANS, AND WOULD ALWAYS BE BEYOND HIS REACH.
XIWANGMU ASKED MU TO STAY AND REST BEFORE HE DEPARTED, FOR SHE WAS LONELY. MU AGREED, SAYING HE WOULD STAY ONE NIGHT BEFORE HE LEFT.

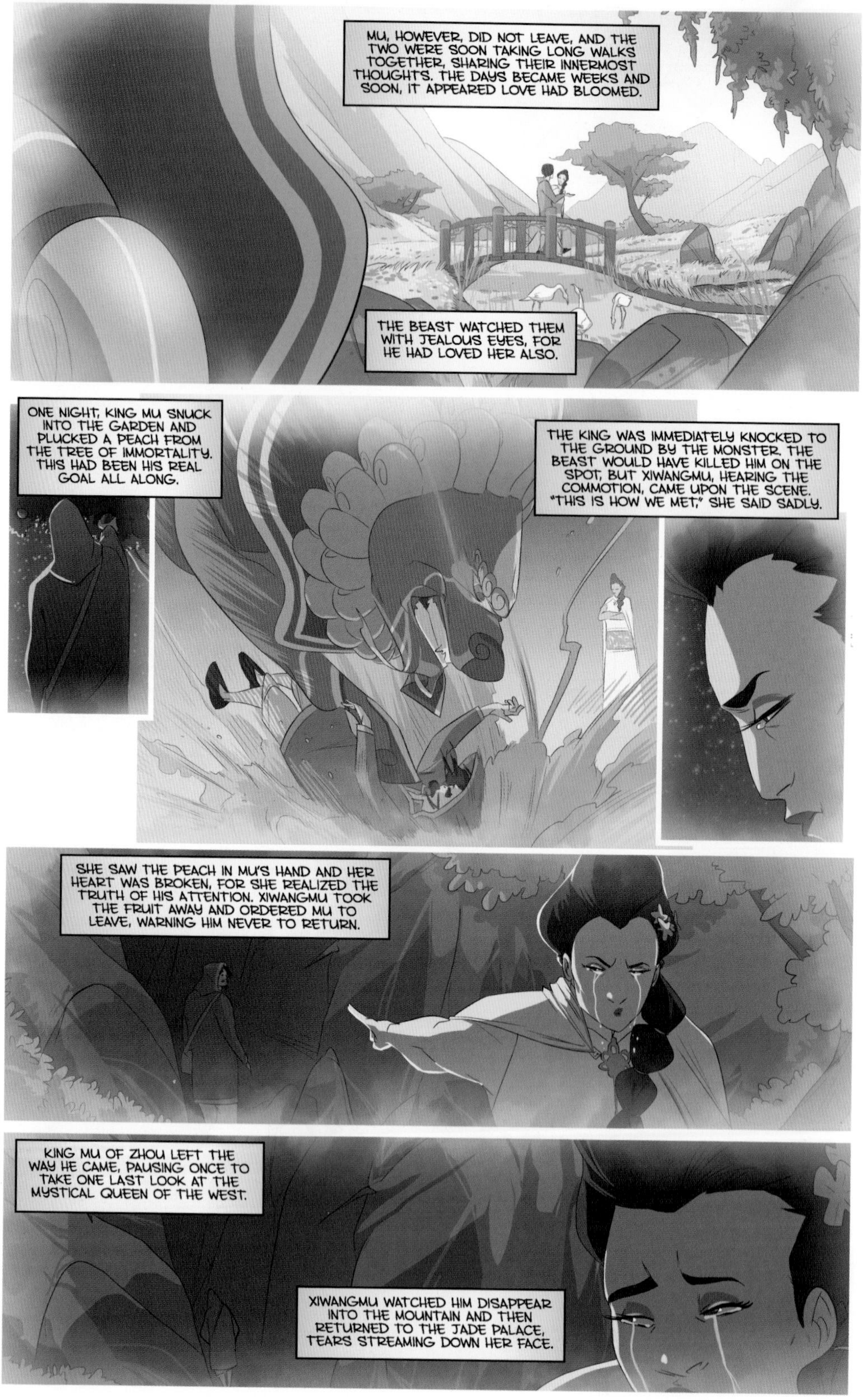
MU, HOWEVER, DID NOT LEAVE, AND THE TWO WERE SOON TAKING LONG WALKS TOGETHER, SHARING THEIR INNERMOST THOUGHTS. THE DAYS BECAME WEEKS AND SOON, IT APPEARED LOVE HAD BLOOMED.
THE BEAST WATCHED THEM WITH JEALOUS EYES, FOR HE HAD LOVED HER ALSO.
ONE NIGHT, KING MU SNUCK INTO THE GARDEN AND PLUCKED A PEACH FROM THE TREE OF IMMORTALITY. THIS HAD BEEN HIS REAL GOAL ALL ALONG.
THE KING WAS IMMEDIATELY KNOCKED TO THE GROUND BY THE MONSTER. THE BEAST WOULD HAVE KILLED HIM ON THE SPOT, BUT XIWANGMU, HEARING THE COMMOTION, CAME UPON THE SCENE. "THIS IS HOW WE MET," SHE SAID SADLY.
SHE SAW THE PEACH IN MU'S HAND AND HER HEART WAS BROKEN, FOR SHE REALIZED THE TRUTH OF HIS ATTENTION. XIWANGMU TOOK THE FRUIT AWAY AND ORDERED MU TO LEAVE, WARNING HIM NEVER TO RETURN.
KING MU OF ZHOU LEFT THE WAY HE CAME, PAUSING ONCE TO TAKE ONE LAST LOOK AT THE MYSTICAL QUEEN OF THE WEST.
XIWANGMU WATCHED HIM DISAPPEAR INTO THE MOUNTAIN AND THEN RETURNED TO THE JADE PALACE, TEARS STREAMING DOWN HER FACE.

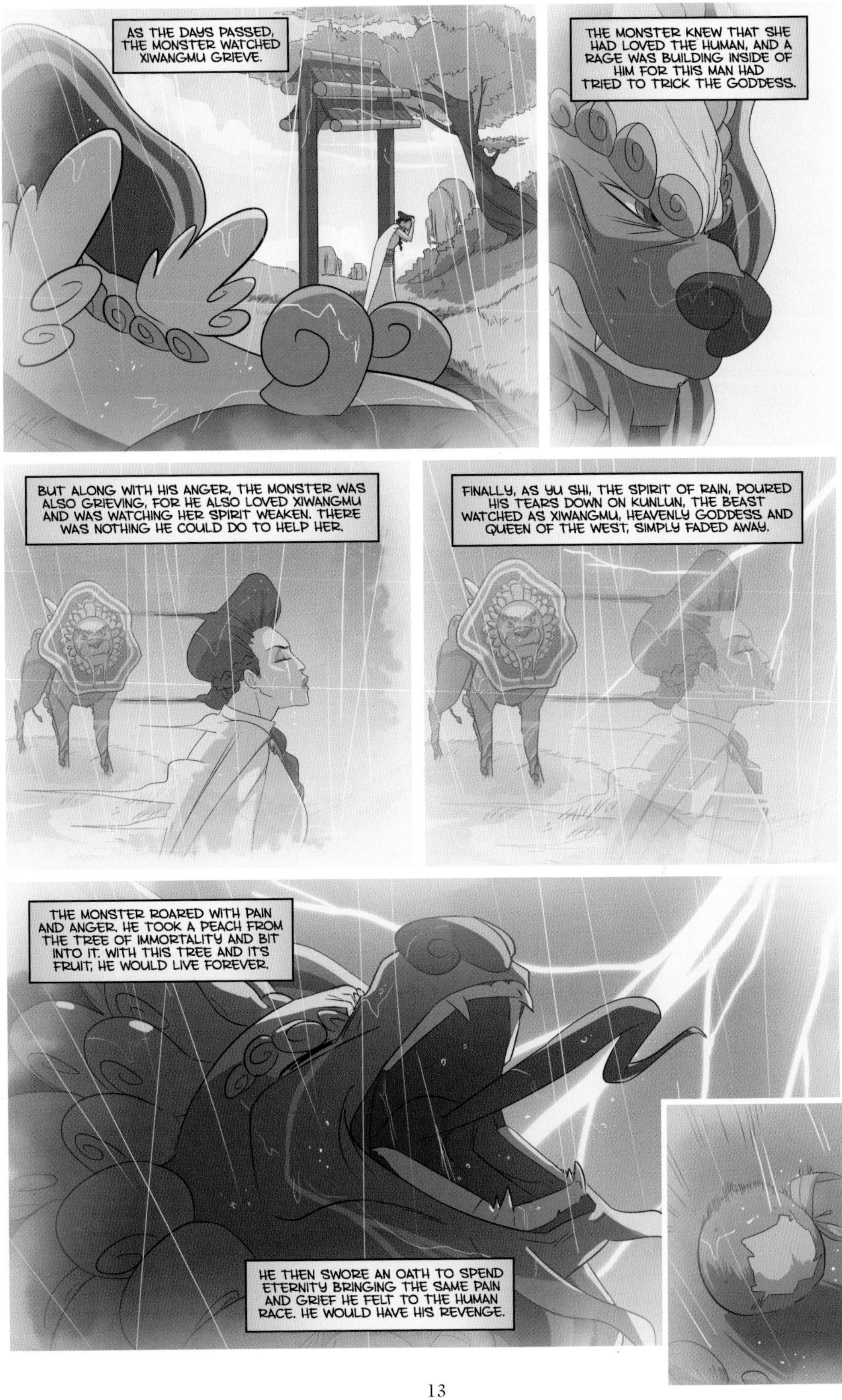
AS THE DAYS PASSED, THE MONSTER WATCHED XIWANGMU GRIEVE.
THE MONSTER KNEW THAT SHE HAD LOVED THE HUMAN, AND A RAGE WAS BUILDING INSIDE OF HIM FOR THIS MAN HAD TRIED TO TRICK THE GODDESS.
BUT ALONG WITH HIS ANGER, THE MONSTER WAS ALSO GRIEVING, FOR HE ALSO LOVED XIWANGMU AND WAS WATCHING HER SPIRIT WEAKEN. THERE WAS NOTHING HE COULD DO TO HELP HER.
FINALLY, AS YU SHI, THE SPIRIT OF RAIN, POURED HIS TEARS DOWN ON KUNLUN, THE BEAST WATCHED AS XIWANGMU, HEAVENLY GODDESS AND QUEEN OF THE WEST, SIMPLY FADED AWAY.
THE MONSTER ROARED WITH PAIN AND ANGER. HE TOOK A PEACH FROM THE TREE OF IMMORTALITY AND BIT INTO IT. WITH THIS TREE AND ITS FRUIT, HE WOULD LIVE FOREVER.
HE THEN SWORE AN OATH TO SPEND ETERNITY BRINGING THE SAME PAIN AND GRIEF HE FELT TO THE HUMAN RACE. HE WOULD HAVE HIS REVENGE.

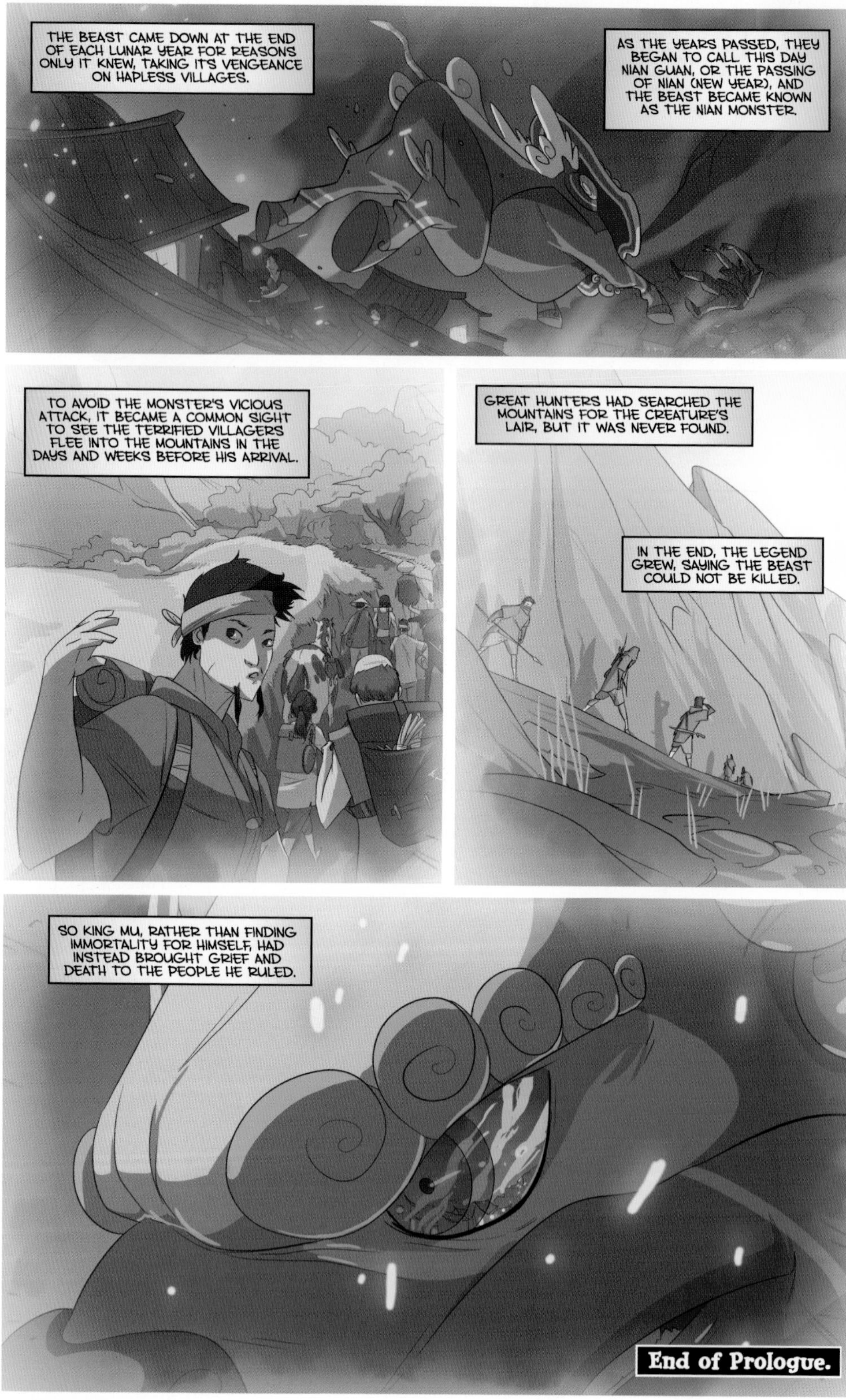
THE BEAST CAME DOWN AT THE END OF EACH LUNAR YEAR FOR REASONS ONLY IT KNEW, TAKING IT'S VENGEANCE ON HAPLESS VILLAGES.
AS THE YEARS PASSED, THEY BEGAN TO CALL THIS DAY NIAN GUAN, OR THE PASSING OF NIAN (NEW YEAR), AND THE BEAST BECAME KNOWN AS THE NIAN MONSTER.
TO AVOID THE MONSTER'S VICIOUS ATTACK, IT BECAME A COMMON SIGHT TO SEE THE TERRIFIED VILLAGERS FLEE INTO THE MOUNTAINS IN THE DAYS AND WEEKS BEFORE HIS ARRIVAL.
GREAT HUNTERS HAD SEARCHED THE MOUNTAINS FOR THE CREATURE'S LAIR, BUT IT WAS NEVER FOUND.
IN THE END, THE LEGEND GREW, SAYING THE BEAST COULD NOT BE KILLED.
SO KING MU, RATHER THAN FINDING IMMORTALITY FOR HIMSELF, HAD INSTEAD BROUGHT GRIEF AND DEATH TO THE PEOPLE HE RULED.
End of Prologue.

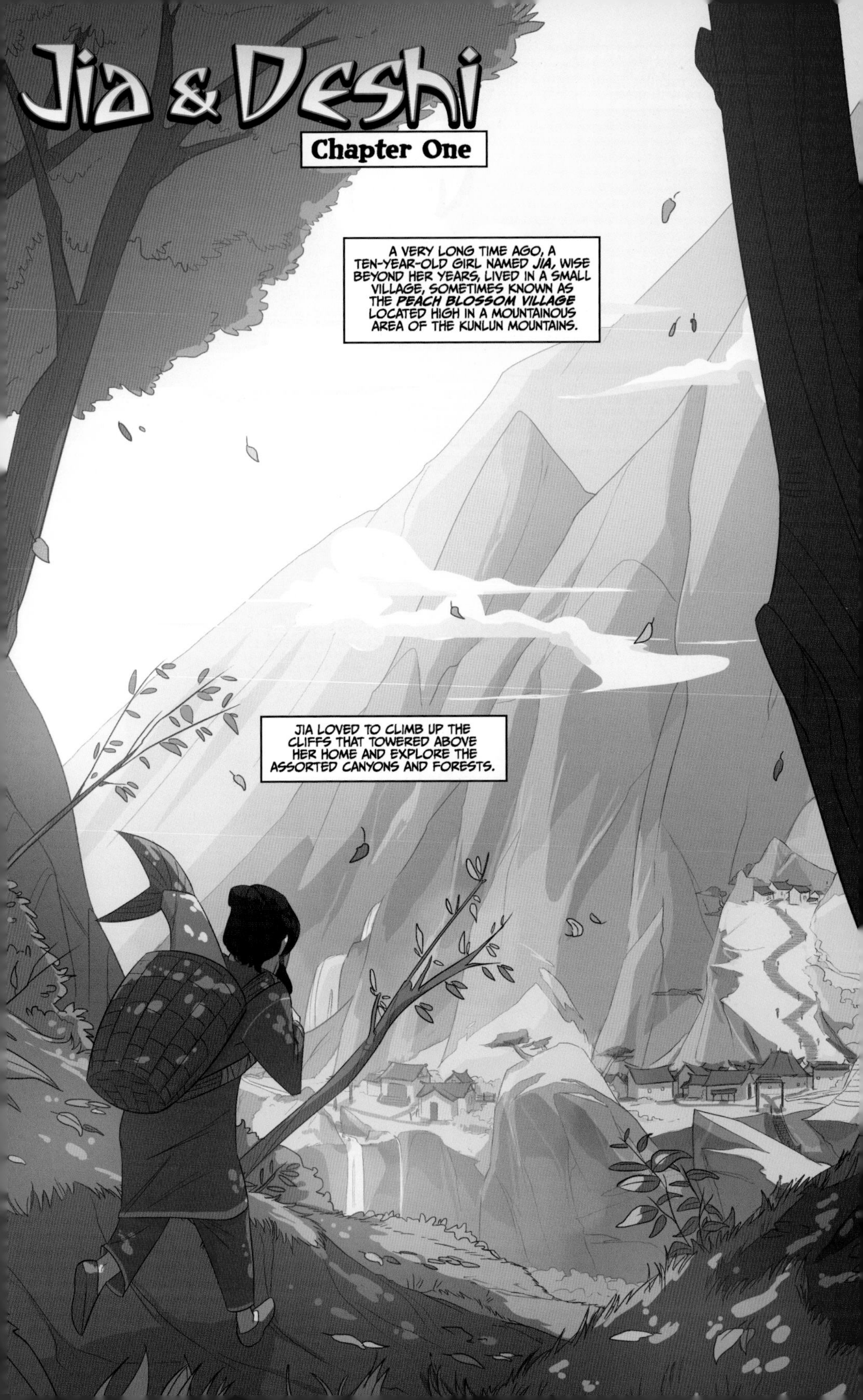
Jia & Deshi
Chapter One
A VERY LONG TIME AGO, A TEN-YEAR-OLD GIRL NAMED JIA, WISE BEYOND HER YEARS, LIVED IN A SMALL VILLAGE, SOMETIMES KNOWN AS THE PEACH BLOSSOM VILLAGE LOCATED HIGH IN A MOUNTAINOUS AREA OF THE KUNLUN MOUNTAINS.
JIA LOVED TO CLIMB UP THE CLIFFS THAT TOWERED ABOVE HER HOME AND EXPLORE THE ASSORTED CANYONS AND FORESTS.

THE ANIMALS KNOW HER WELL AND IT EVEN SEEMS AS THOUGH THEY UNDERSTAND HER WHEN SHE TALKS WITH THEM.

GOOD AFTERNOON, DEER.

THE VILLAGERS ALL KNEW JIA WELL, FOR SHE ALWAYS SEEMED TO BE GETTING INTO MISCHIEF. SHE HAD A WAY OF WINNING THEM OVER, HOWEVER, WITH A SMILE AND HER CHEERFUL NATURE.

HELLO, JIA. I SEE YOU'VE CAUGHT ANOTHER FISH! YOU ARE AN *AMAZING* YOUNG LADY.

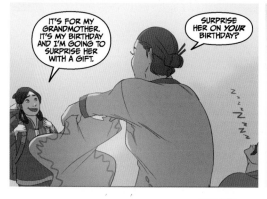

IT'S FOR MY GRANDMOTHER. IT'S MY BIRTHDAY AND I'M GOING TO SURPRISE HER WITH A GIFT.

SURPRISE HER ON *YOUR* BIRTHDAY?

BUT THAT'S THE THIRD FISH YOU'VE CAUGHT THIS WEEK, I DOUBT YOU WILL SURPRISE HER.

YES, BUT THIS IS THE BIGGEST FISH YET. BESIDES, GRANDMOTHER IS *ALWAYS* SURPRISED WHEN I BRING A FISH HOME.

YES, I SUPPOSE SHE IS. MAYBE YOU COULD TEACH MY HUSBAND HOW TO FISH.

HEY...

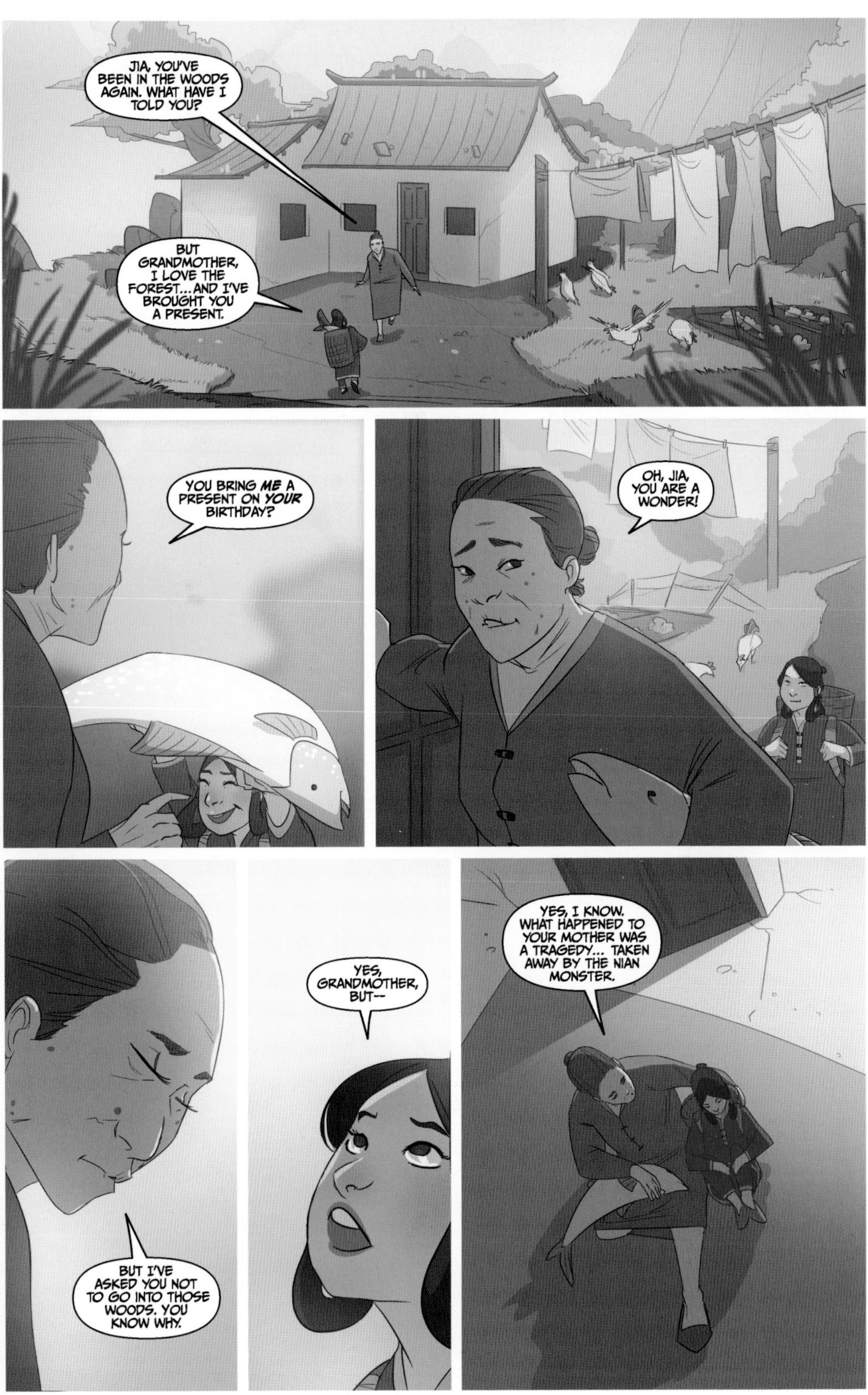
JIA, YOU'VE BEEN IN THE WOODS AGAIN. WHAT HAVE I TOLD YOU?
BUT GRANDMOTHER, I LOVE THE FOREST...AND I'VE BROUGHT YOU A PRESENT.
YOU BRING ME A PRESENT ON YOUR BIRTHDAY?
OH, JIA, YOU ARE A WONDER!
BUT I'VE ASKED YOU NOT TO GO INTO THOSE WOODS. YOU KNOW WHY.
YES, GRANDMOTHER, BUT--
YES, I KNOW. WHAT HAPPENED TO YOUR MOTHER WAS A TRAGEDY... TAKEN AWAY BY THE NIAN MONSTER.

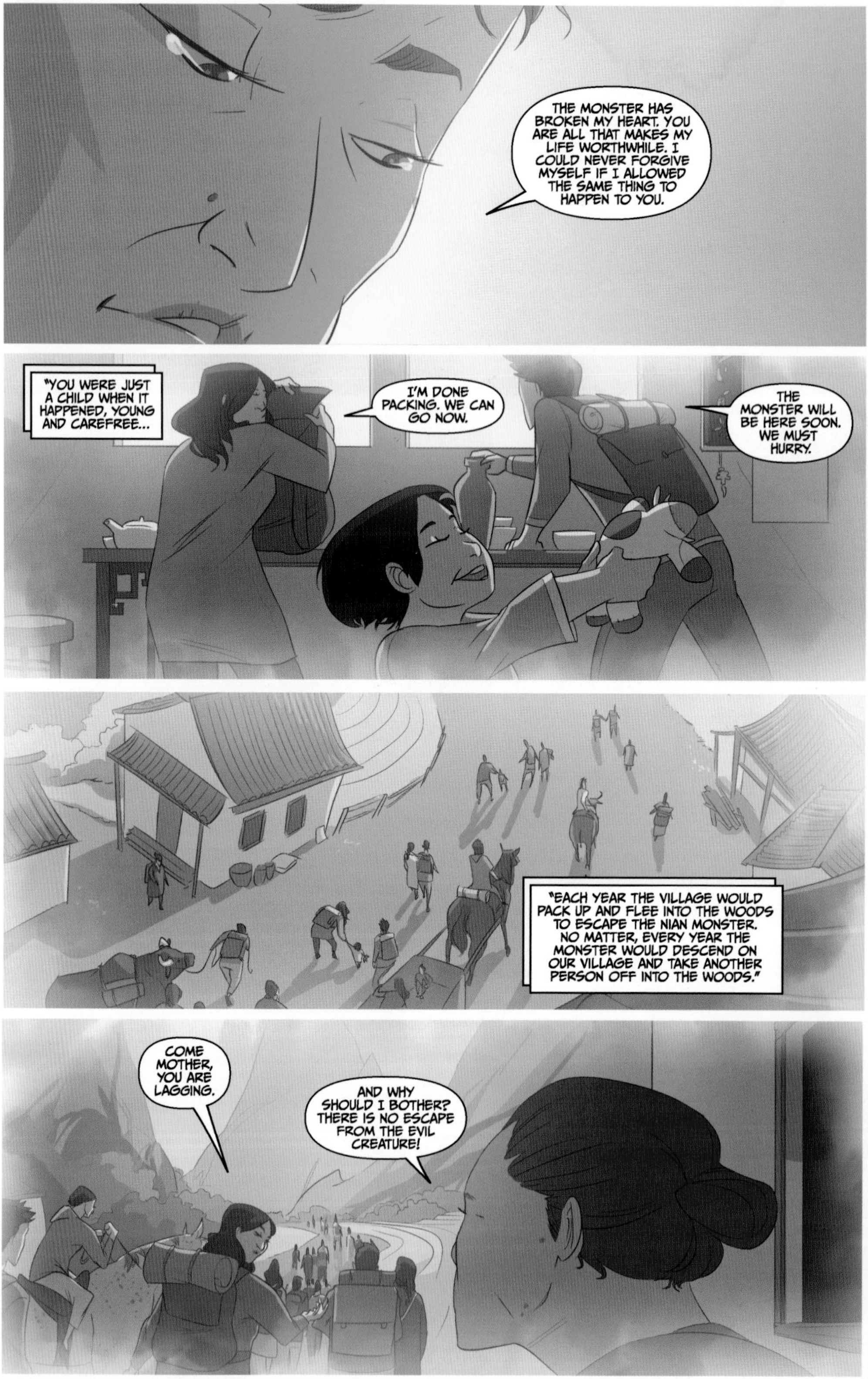
THE MONSTER HAS BROKEN MY HEART. YOU ARE ALL THAT MAKES MY LIFE WORTHWHILE. I COULD NEVER FORGIVE MYSELF IF I ALLOWED THE SAME THING TO HAPPEN TO YOU.
"YOU WERE JUST A CHILD WHEN IT HAPPENED, YOUNG AND CAREFREE...
I'M DONE PACKING. WE CAN GO NOW.
THE MONSTER WILL BE HERE SOON. WE MUST HURRY.
"EACH YEAR THE VILLAGE WOULD PACK UP AND FLEE INTO THE WOODS TO ESCAPE THE NIAN MONSTER. NO MATTER, EVERY YEAR THE MONSTER WOULD DESCEND ON OUR VILLAGE AND TAKE ANOTHER PERSON OFF INTO THE WOODS."
COME MOTHER, YOU ARE LAGGING.
AND WHY SHOULD I BOTHER? THERE IS NO ESCAPE FROM THE EVIL CREATURE!

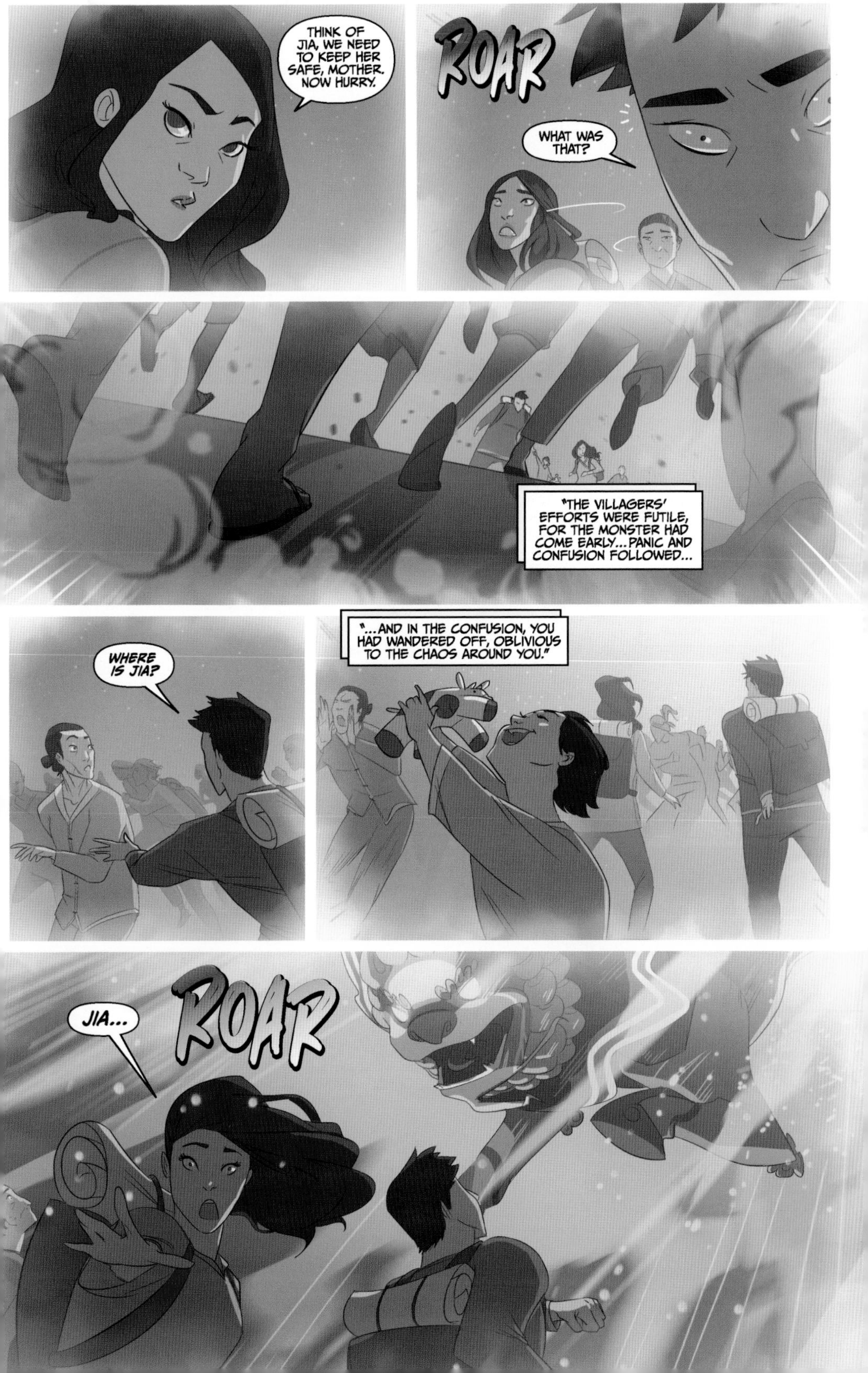
THINK OF JIA, WE NEED TO KEEP HER SAFE, MOTHER. NOW HURRY.
ROAR
WHAT WAS THAT?
"THE VILLAGERS' EFFORTS WERE FUTILE, FOR THE MONSTER HAD COME EARLY...PANIC AND CONFUSION FOLLOWED...
WHERE IS JIA?
"...AND IN THE CONFUSION, YOU HAD WANDERED OFF, OBLIVIOUS TO THE CHAOS AROUND YOU."
JIA...
ROAR

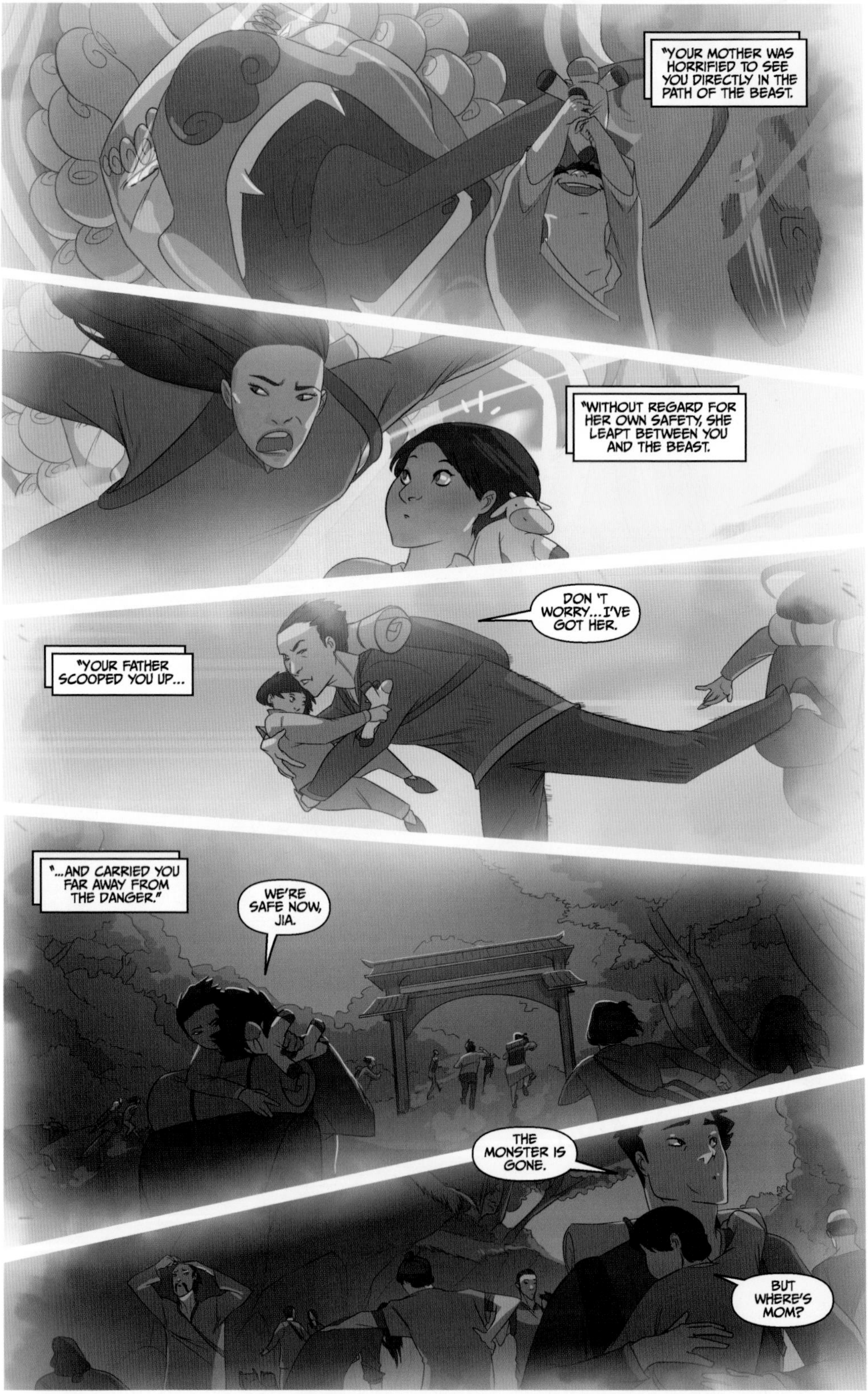
"YOUR MOTHER WAS HORRIFIED TO SEE YOU DIRECTLY IN THE PATH OF THE BEAST.
"WITHOUT REGARD FOR HER OWN SAFETY, SHE LEAPT BETWEEN YOU AND THE BEAST.
"YOUR FATHER SCOOPED YOU UP...
DON'T WORRY... I'VE GOT HER.
"...AND CARRIED YOU FAR AWAY FROM THE DANGER."
WE'RE SAFE NOW, JIA.
THE MONSTER IS GONE.
BUT WHERE'S MOM?

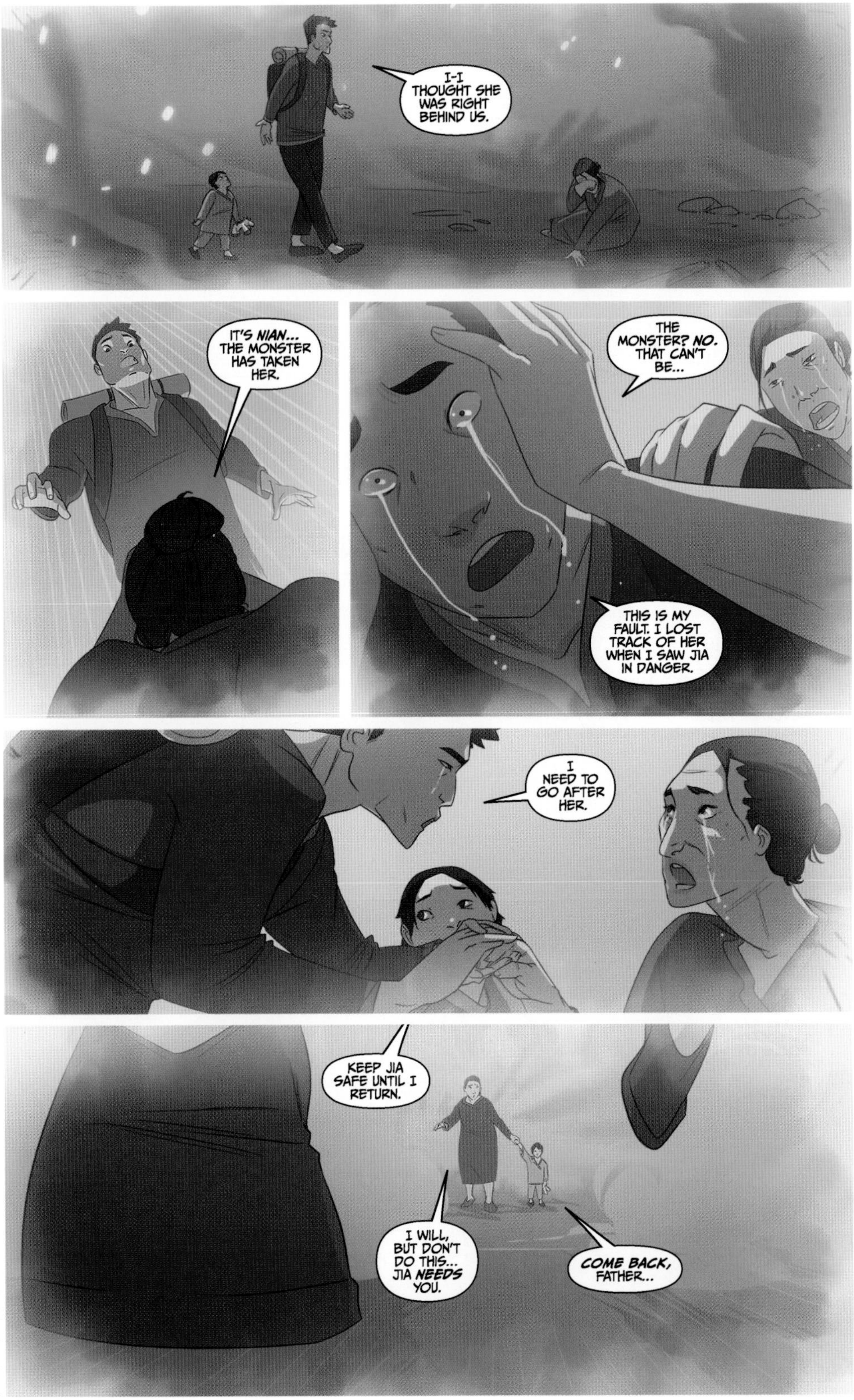
I-I THOUGHT SHE WAS RIGHT BEHIND US.
IT'S NIAN... THE MONSTER HAS TAKEN HER.
THE MONSTER? NO. THAT CAN'T BE...
THIS IS MY FAULT. I LOST TRACK OF HER WHEN I SAW JIA IN DANGER.
I NEED TO GO AFTER HER.
KEEP JIA SAFE UNTIL I RETURN.
I WILL, BUT DON'T DO THIS... JIA NEEDS YOU.
COME BACK, FATHER...

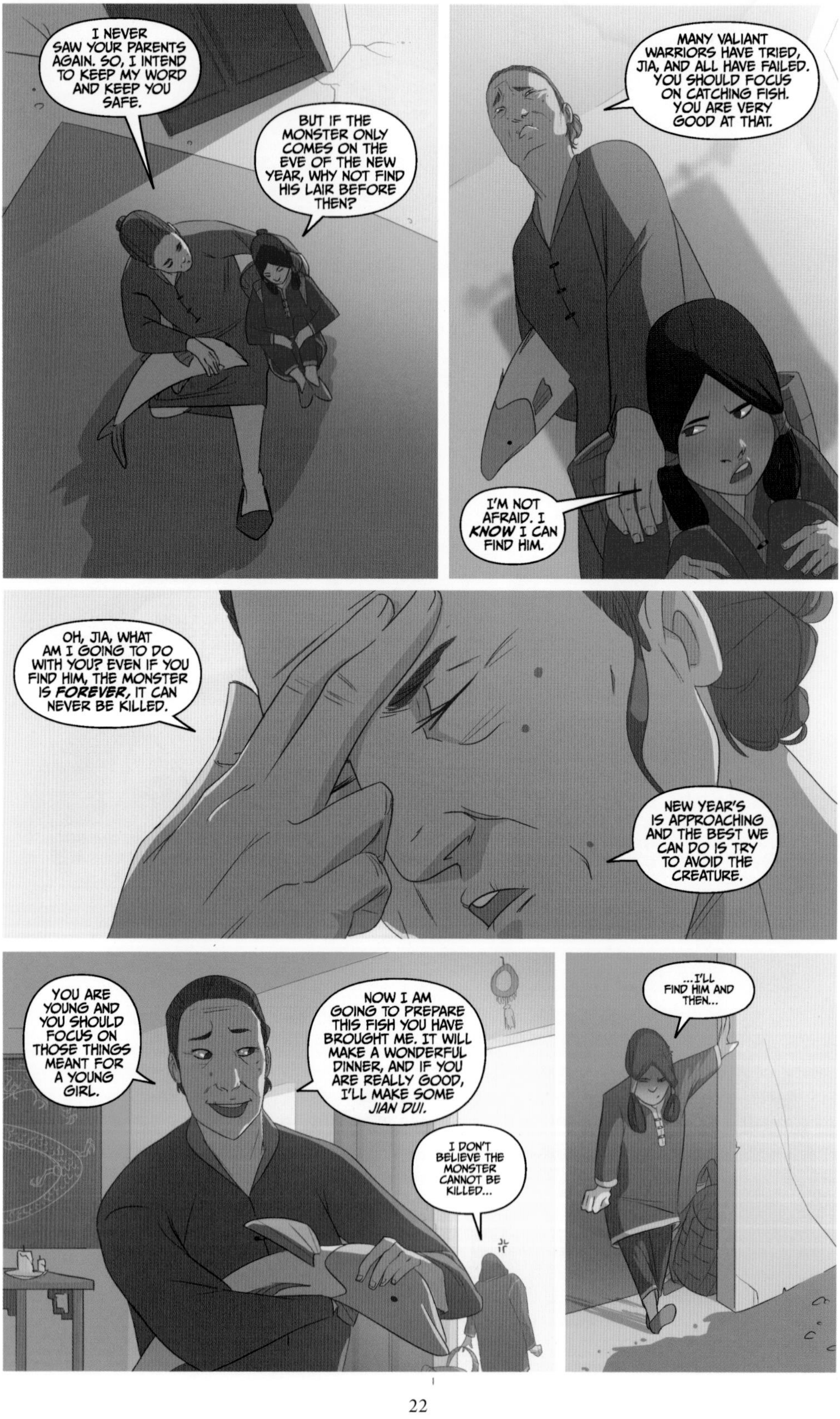
I NEVER SAW YOUR PARENTS AGAIN. SO, I INTEND TO KEEP MY WORD AND KEEP YOU SAFE.
BUT IF THE MONSTER ONLY COMES ON THE EVE OF THE NEW YEAR, WHY NOT FIND HIS LAIR BEFORE THEN?
MANY VALIANT WARRIORS HAVE TRIED, JIA, AND ALL HAVE FAILED. YOU SHOULD FOCUS ON CATCHING FISH. YOU ARE VERY GOOD AT THAT.
I'M NOT AFRAID. I *KNOW* I CAN FIND HIM.
OH, JIA, WHAT AM I GOING TO DO WITH YOU? EVEN IF YOU FIND HIM, THE MONSTER IS *FOREVER,* IT CAN NEVER BE KILLED.
NEW YEAR'S IS APPROACHING AND THE BEST WE CAN DO IS TRY TO AVOID THE CREATURE.
YOU ARE YOUNG AND YOU SHOULD FOCUS ON THOSE THINGS MEANT FOR A YOUNG GIRL.
NOW I AM GOING TO PREPARE THIS FISH YOU HAVE BROUGHT ME. IT WILL MAKE A WONDERFUL DINNER, AND IF YOU ARE REALLY GOOD, I'LL MAKE SOME *JIAN DUI.*
I DON'T BELIEVE THE MONSTER CANNOT BE KILLED...
...I'LL FIND HIM AND THEN...

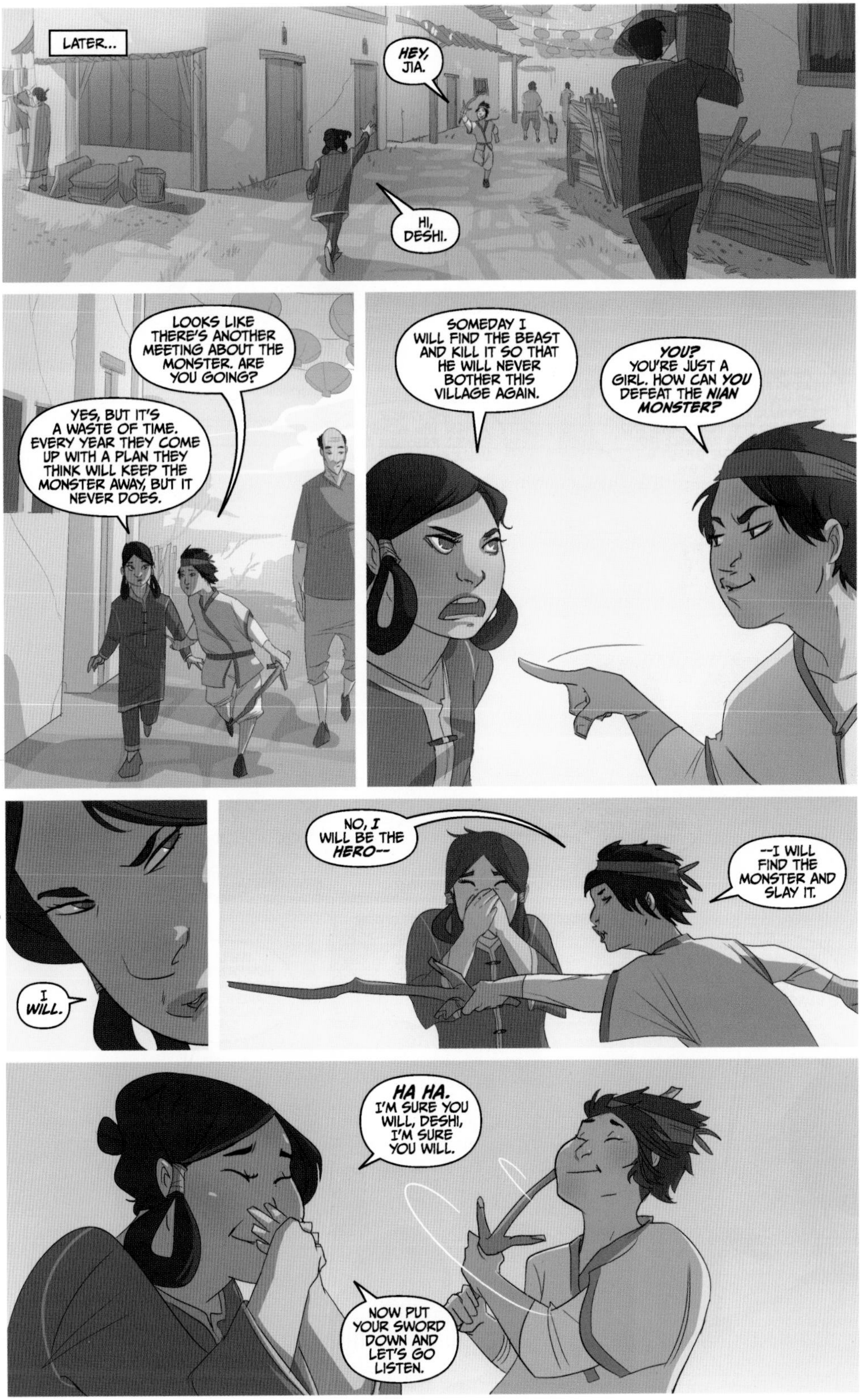
LATER...
HEY, JIA.
HI, DESHI.
LOOKS LIKE THERE'S ANOTHER MEETING ABOUT THE MONSTER. ARE YOU GOING?
YES, BUT IT'S A WASTE OF TIME. EVERY YEAR THEY COME UP WITH A PLAN THEY THINK WILL KEEP THE MONSTER AWAY, BUT IT NEVER DOES.
SOMEDAY I WILL FIND THE BEAST AND KILL IT SO THAT HE WILL NEVER BOTHER THIS VILLAGE AGAIN.
YOU? YOU'RE JUST A GIRL. HOW CAN YOU DEFEAT THE NIAN MONSTER?
I WILL.
NO, I WILL BE THE HERO--
--I WILL FIND THE MONSTER AND SLAY IT.
HA HA. I'M SURE YOU WILL, DESHI, I'M SURE YOU WILL.
NOW PUT YOUR SWORD DOWN AND LET'S GO LISTEN.

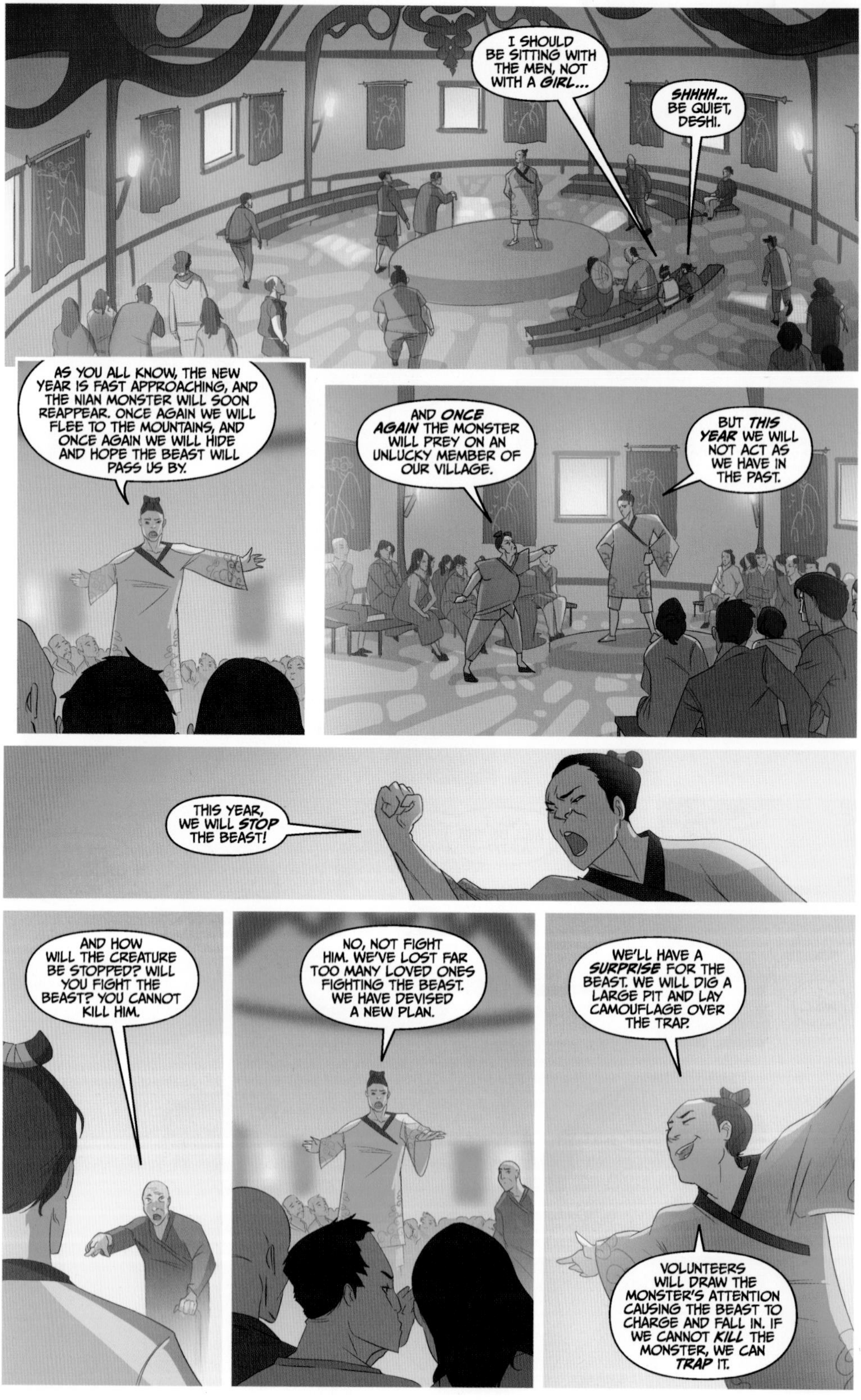
I SHOULD BE SITTING WITH THE MEN, NOT WITH A GIRL...
SHHHH... BE QUIET, DESHI.
AS YOU ALL KNOW, THE NEW YEAR IS FAST APPROACHING, AND THE NIAN MONSTER WILL SOON REAPPEAR. ONCE AGAIN WE WILL FLEE TO THE MOUNTAINS, AND ONCE AGAIN WE WILL HIDE AND HOPE THE BEAST WILL PASS US BY.
AND ONCE AGAIN THE MONSTER WILL PREY ON AN UNLUCKY MEMBER OF OUR VILLAGE.
BUT THIS YEAR WE WILL NOT ACT AS WE HAVE IN THE PAST.
THIS YEAR, WE WILL STOP THE BEAST!
AND HOW WILL THE CREATURE BE STOPPED? WILL YOU FIGHT THE BEAST? YOU CANNOT KILL HIM.
NO, NOT FIGHT HIM. WE'VE LOST FAR TOO MANY LOVED ONES FIGHTING THE BEAST. WE HAVE DEVISED A NEW PLAN.
WE'LL HAVE A SURPRISE FOR THE BEAST. WE WILL DIG A LARGE PIT AND LAY CAMOUFLAGE OVER THE TRAP.
VOLUNTEERS WILL DRAW THE MONSTER'S ATTENTION CAUSING THE BEAST TO CHARGE AND FALL IN. IF WE CANNOT KILL THE MONSTER, WE CAN TRAP IT.

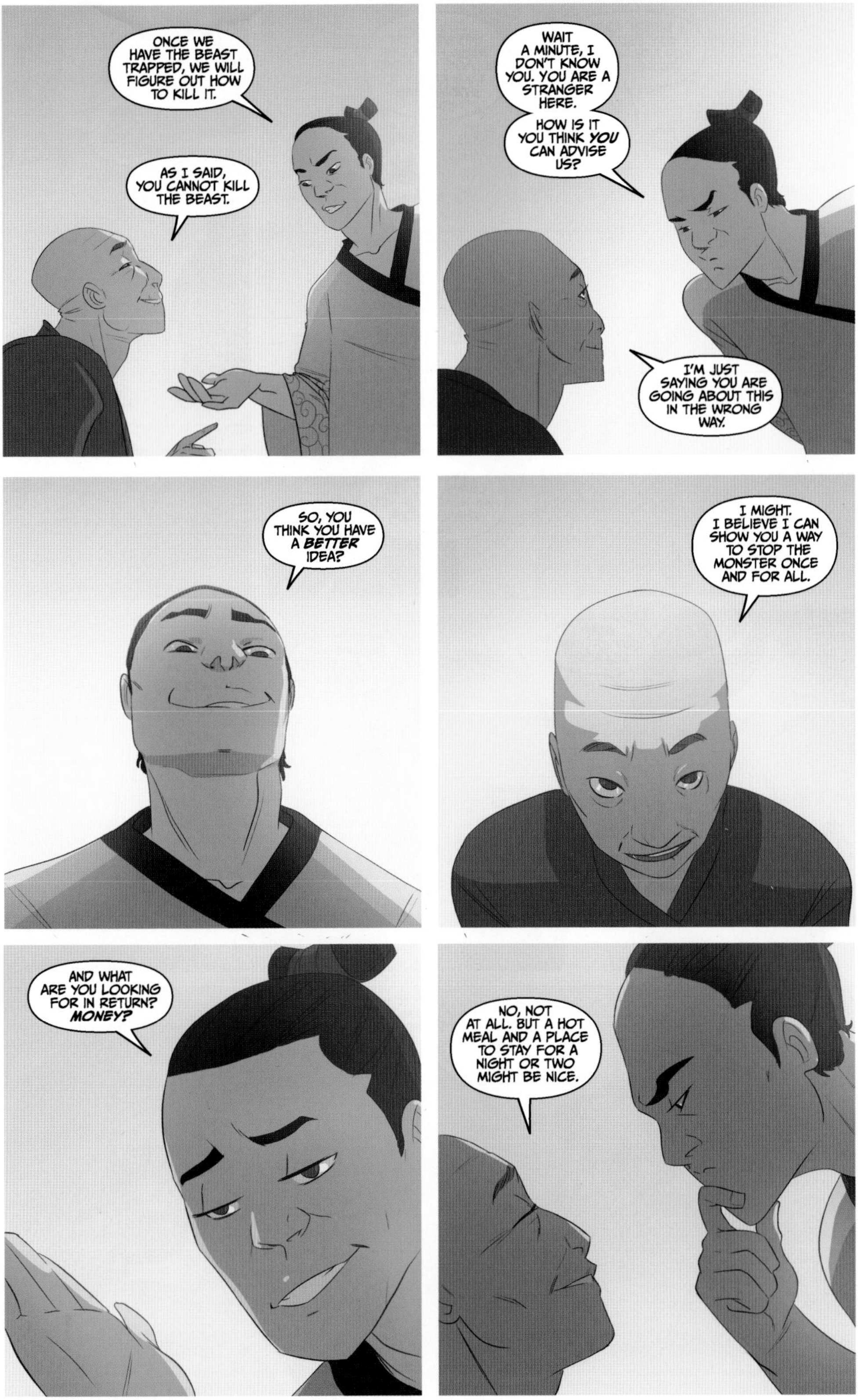
ONCE WE HAVE THE BEAST TRAPPED, WE WILL FIGURE OUT HOW TO KILL IT.
AS I SAID, YOU CANNOT KILL THE BEAST.
WAIT A MINUTE, I DON'T KNOW YOU. YOU ARE A STRANGER HERE.
HOW IS IT YOU THINK *YOU* CAN ADVISE US?
I'M JUST SAYING YOU ARE GOING ABOUT THIS IN THE WRONG WAY.
SO, YOU THINK YOU HAVE A *BETTER* IDEA?
I MIGHT. I BELIEVE I CAN SHOW YOU A WAY TO STOP THE MONSTER ONCE AND FOR ALL.
AND WHAT ARE YOU LOOKING FOR IN RETURN? *MONEY?*
NO, NOT AT ALL. BUT A HOT MEAL AND A PLACE TO STAY FOR A NIGHT OR TWO MIGHT BE NICE.

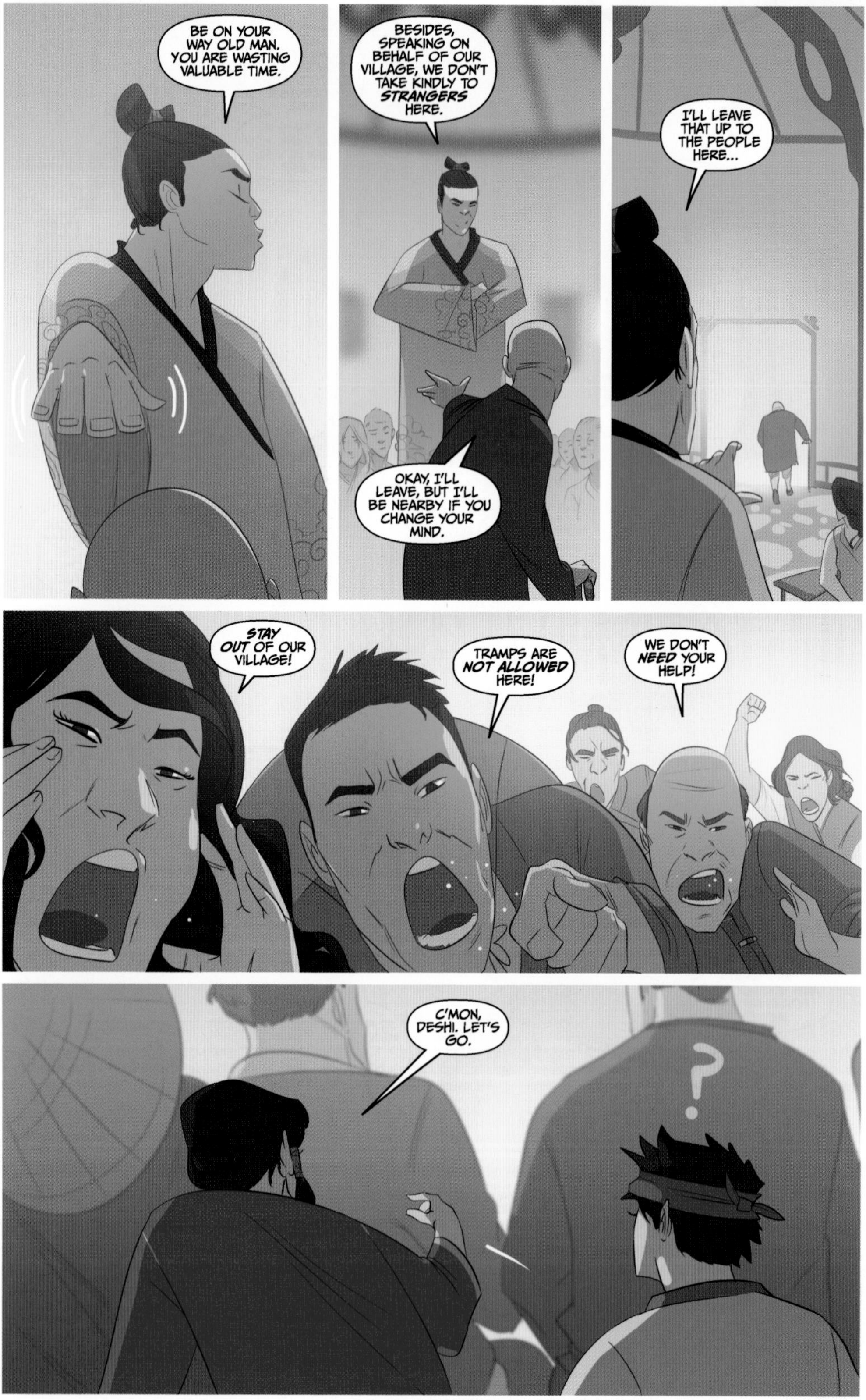
BE ON YOUR WAY OLD MAN. YOU ARE WASTING VALUABLE TIME.
BESIDES, SPEAKING ON BEHALF OF OUR VILLAGE, WE DON'T TAKE KINDLY TO STRANGERS HERE.
OKAY, I'LL LEAVE, BUT I'LL BE NEARBY IF YOU CHANGE YOUR MIND.
I'LL LEAVE THAT UP TO THE PEOPLE HERE...
STAY OUT OF OUR VILLAGE!
TRAMPS ARE NOT ALLOWED HERE!
WE DON'T NEED YOUR HELP!
C'MON, DESHI. LET'S GO.
?

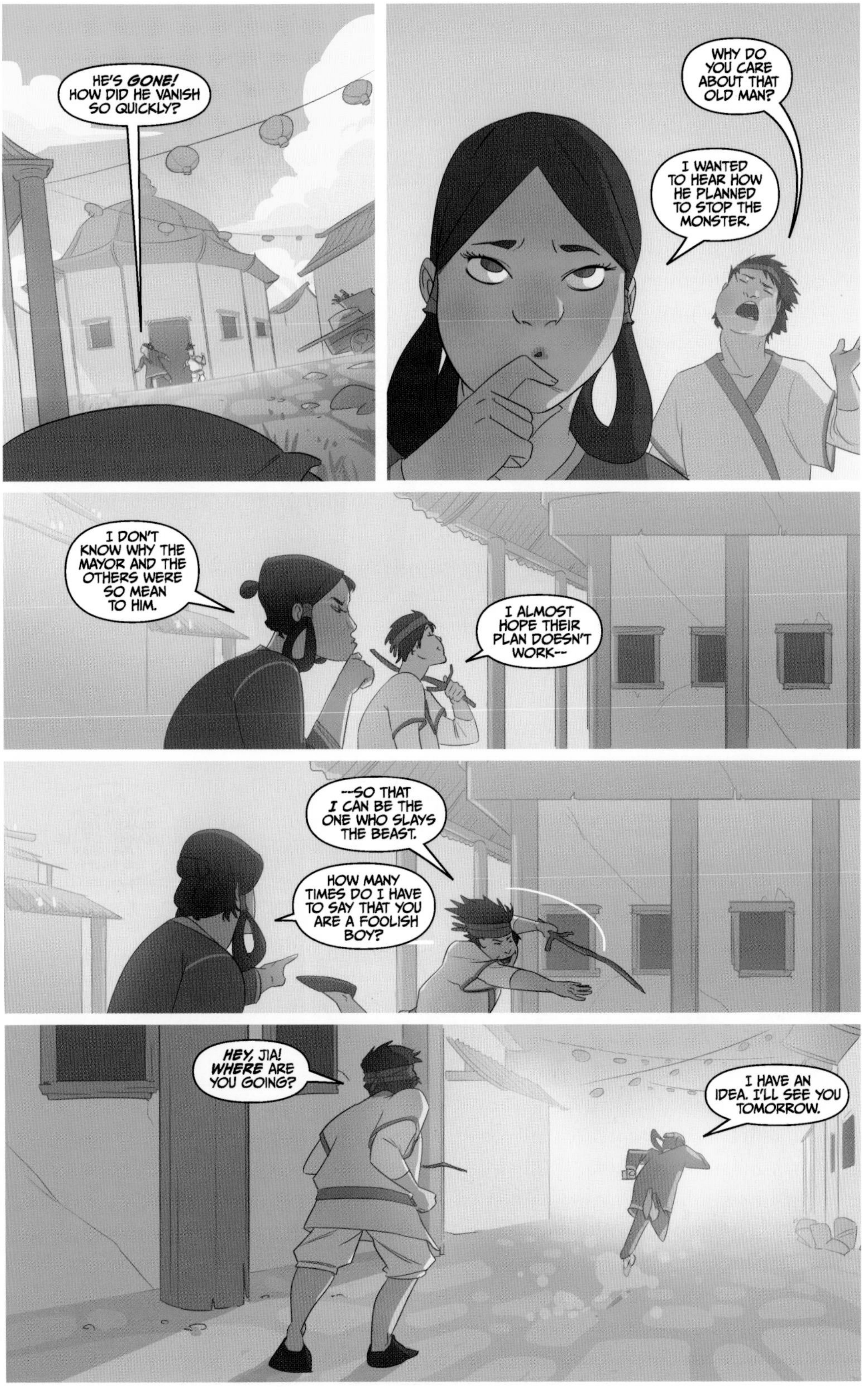
HE'S *GONE!* HOW DID HE VANISH SO QUICKLY?
WHY DO YOU CARE ABOUT THAT OLD MAN?
I WANTED TO HEAR HOW HE PLANNED TO STOP THE MONSTER.
I DON'T KNOW WHY THE MAYOR AND THE OTHERS WERE SO MEAN TO HIM.
I ALMOST HOPE THEIR PLAN DOESN'T WORK--
--SO THAT *I* CAN BE THE ONE WHO SLAYS THE BEAST.
HOW MANY TIMES DO I HAVE TO SAY THAT YOU ARE A FOOLISH BOY?
HEY, JIA! *WHERE* ARE YOU GOING?
I HAVE AN IDEA. I'LL SEE YOU TOMORROW.

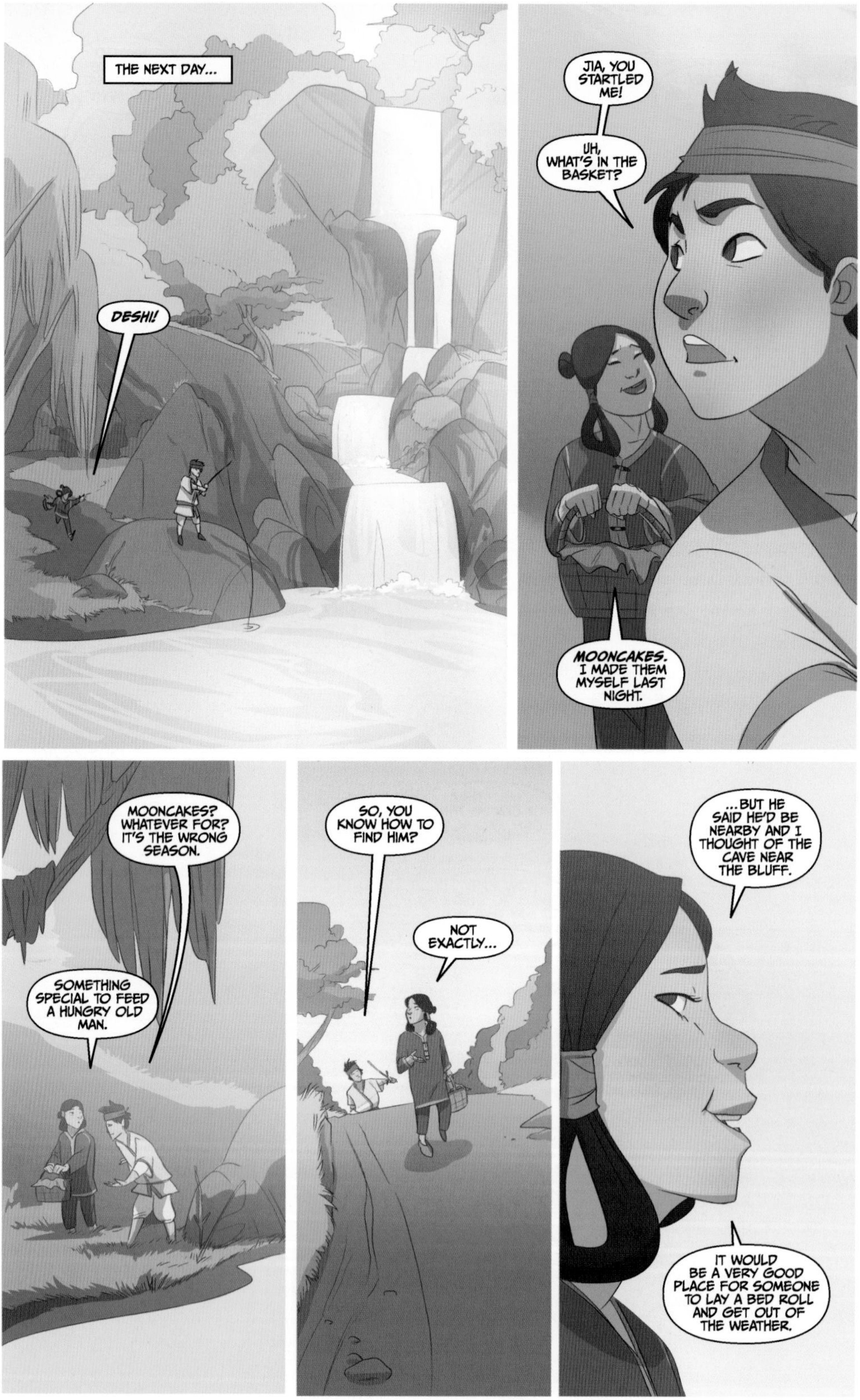
THE NEXT DAY...
DESHI!
JIA, YOU STARTLED ME!
UH, WHAT'S IN THE BASKET?
MOONCAKES. I MADE THEM MYSELF LAST NIGHT.
MOONCAKES? WHATEVER FOR? IT'S THE WRONG SEASON.
SOMETHING SPECIAL TO FEED A HUNGRY OLD MAN.
SO, YOU KNOW HOW TO FIND HIM?
NOT EXACTLY...
...BUT HE SAID HE'D BE NEARBY AND I THOUGHT OF THE CAVE NEAR THE BLUFF.
IT WOULD BE A VERY GOOD PLACE FOR SOMEONE TO LAY A BED ROLL AND GET OUT OF THE WEATHER.

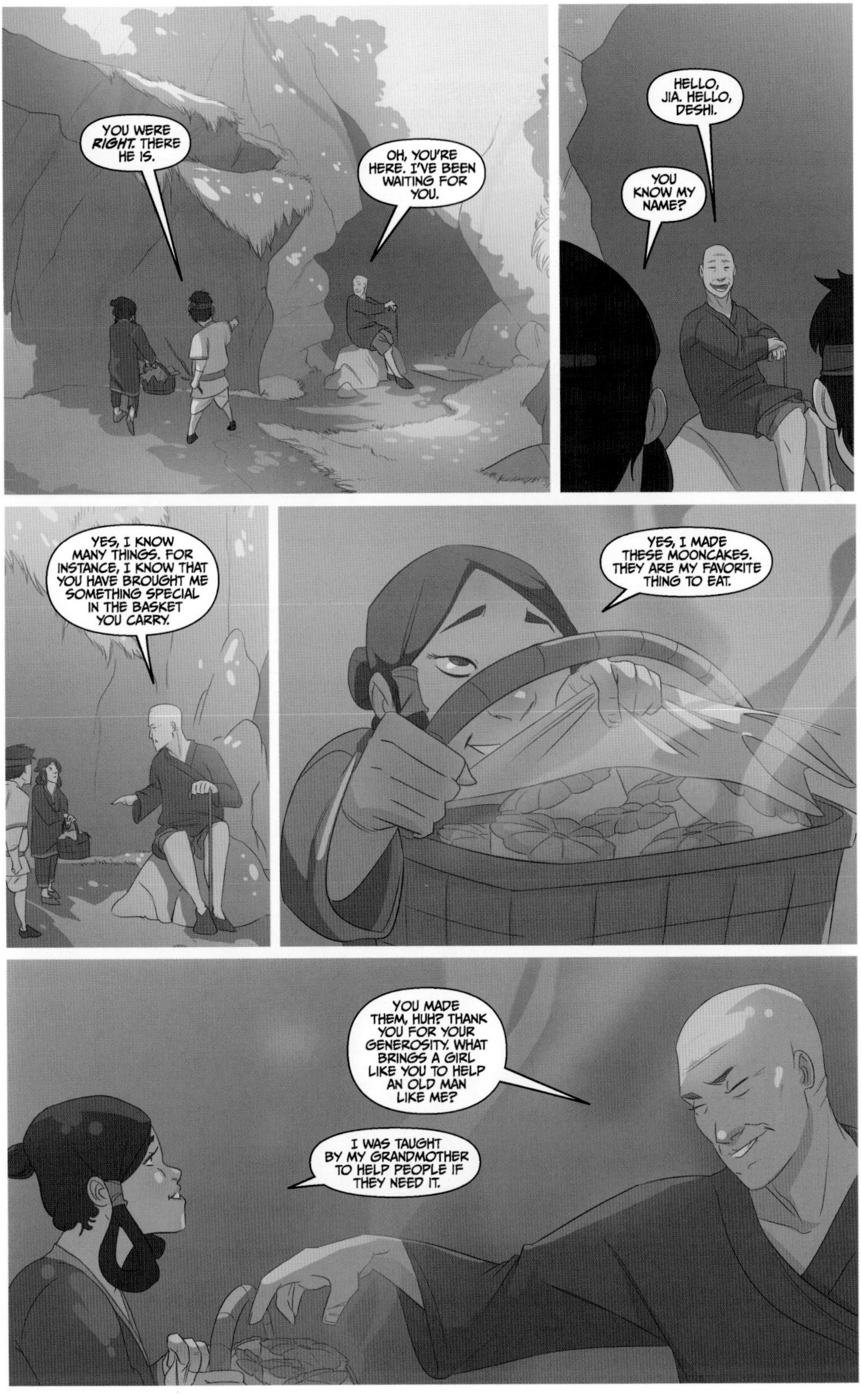
YOU WERE RIGHT. THERE HE IS.
OH, YOU'RE HERE. I'VE BEEN WAITING FOR YOU.
HELLO, JIA. HELLO, DESHI.
YOU KNOW MY NAME?
YES, I KNOW MANY THINGS. FOR INSTANCE, I KNOW THAT YOU HAVE BROUGHT ME SOMETHING SPECIAL IN THE BASKET YOU CARRY.
YES, I MADE THESE MOONCAKES. THEY ARE MY FAVORITE THING TO EAT.
YOU MADE THEM, HUH? THANK YOU FOR YOUR GENEROSITY. WHAT BRINGS A GIRL LIKE YOU TO HELP AN OLD MAN LIKE ME?
I WAS TAUGHT BY MY GRANDMOTHER TO HELP PEOPLE IF THEY NEED IT.

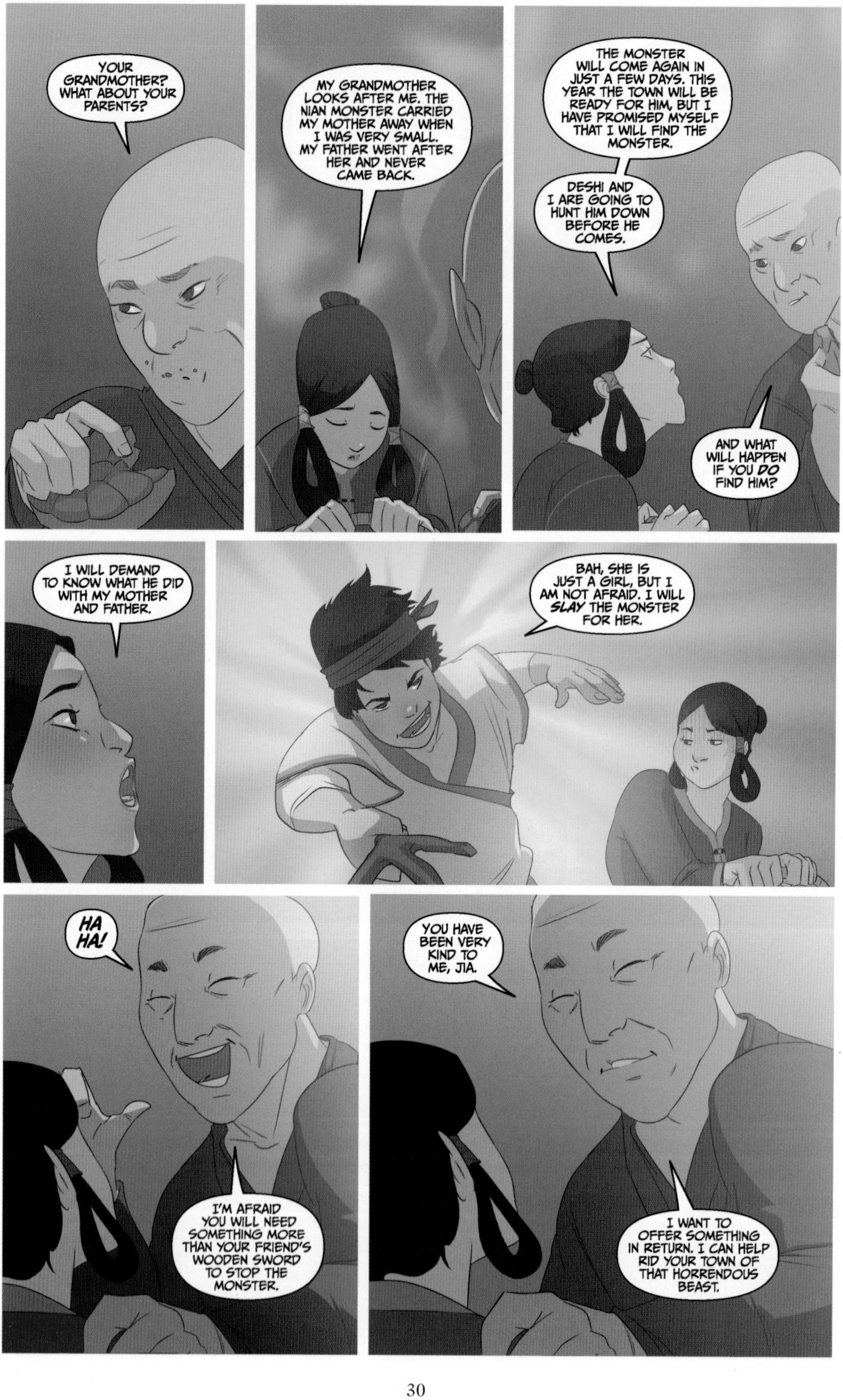
YOUR GRANDMOTHER? WHAT ABOUT YOUR PARENTS?
MY GRANDMOTHER LOOKS AFTER ME. THE NIAN MONSTER CARRIED MY MOTHER AWAY WHEN I WAS VERY SMALL. MY FATHER WENT AFTER HER AND NEVER CAME BACK.
THE MONSTER WILL COME AGAIN IN JUST A FEW DAYS. THIS YEAR THE TOWN WILL BE READY FOR HIM, BUT I HAVE PROMISED MYSELF THAT I WILL FIND THE MONSTER.
DESHI AND I ARE GOING TO HUNT HIM DOWN BEFORE HE COMES.
AND WHAT WILL HAPPEN IF YOU *DO* FIND HIM?
I WILL DEMAND TO KNOW WHAT HE DID WITH MY MOTHER AND FATHER.
BAH, SHE IS JUST A GIRL, BUT I AM NOT AFRAID. I WILL *SLAY* THE MONSTER FOR HER.
HA HA!
I'M AFRAID YOU WILL NEED SOMETHING MORE THAN YOUR FRIEND'S WOODEN SWORD TO STOP THE MONSTER.
YOU HAVE BEEN VERY KIND TO ME, JIA.
I WANT TO OFFER SOMETHING IN RETURN. I CAN HELP RID YOUR TOWN OF THAT HORRENDOUS BEAST.

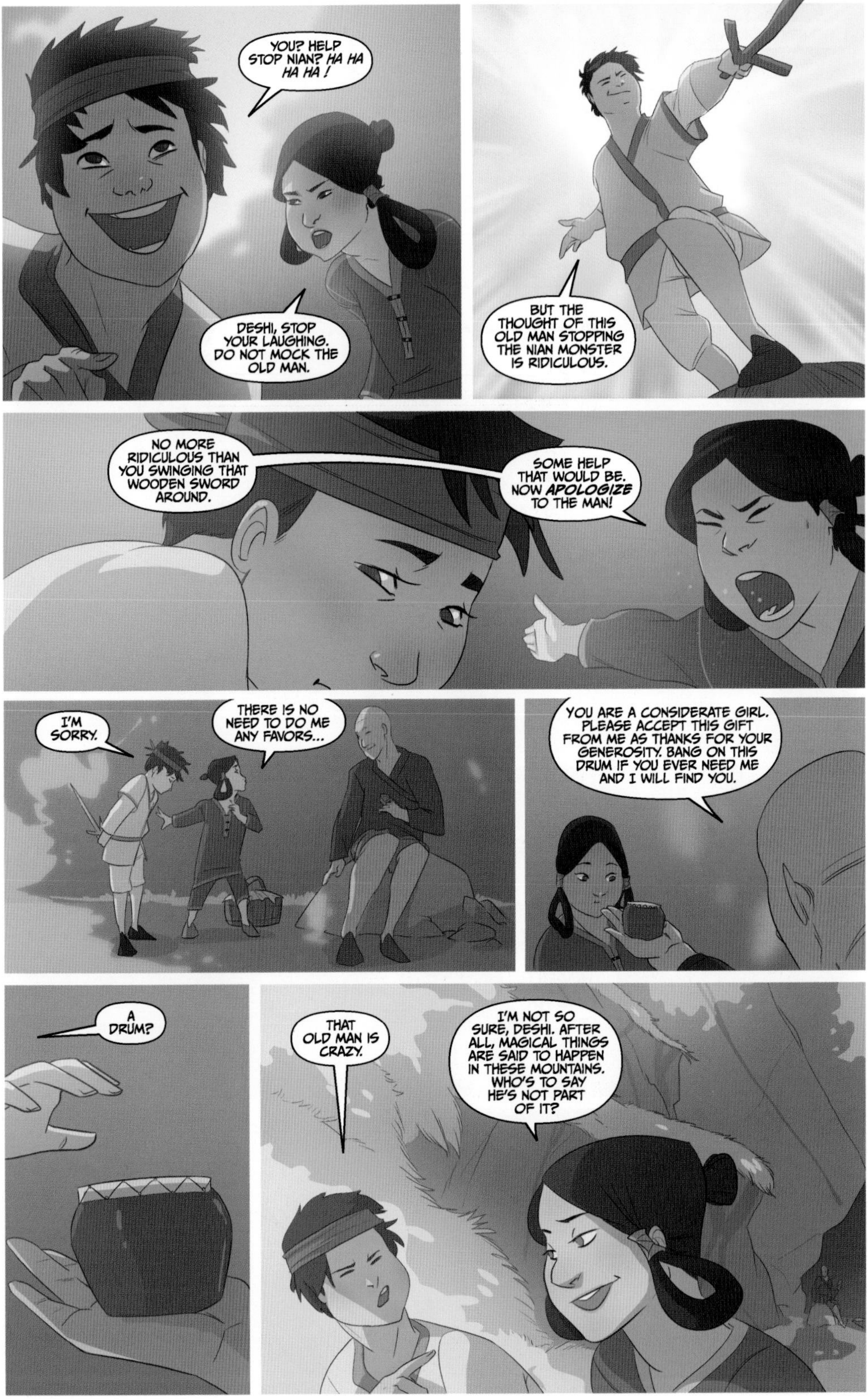
YOU? HELP STOP NIAN? HA HA HA HA!
DESHI, STOP YOUR LAUGHING. DO NOT MOCK THE OLD MAN.
BUT THE THOUGHT OF THIS OLD MAN STOPPING THE NIAN MONSTER IS RIDICULOUS.
NO MORE RIDICULOUS THAN YOU SWINGING THAT WOODEN SWORD AROUND.
SOME HELP THAT WOULD BE. NOW APOLOGIZE TO THE MAN!
I'M SORRY.
THERE IS NO NEED TO DO ME ANY FAVORS...
YOU ARE A CONSIDERATE GIRL. PLEASE ACCEPT THIS GIFT FROM ME AS THANKS FOR YOUR GENEROSITY. BANG ON THIS DRUM IF YOU EVER NEED ME AND I WILL FIND YOU.
A DRUM?
THAT OLD MAN IS CRAZY.
I'M NOT SO SURE, DESHI. AFTER ALL, MAGICAL THINGS ARE SAID TO HAPPEN IN THESE MOUNTAINS. WHO'S TO SAY HE'S NOT PART OF IT?

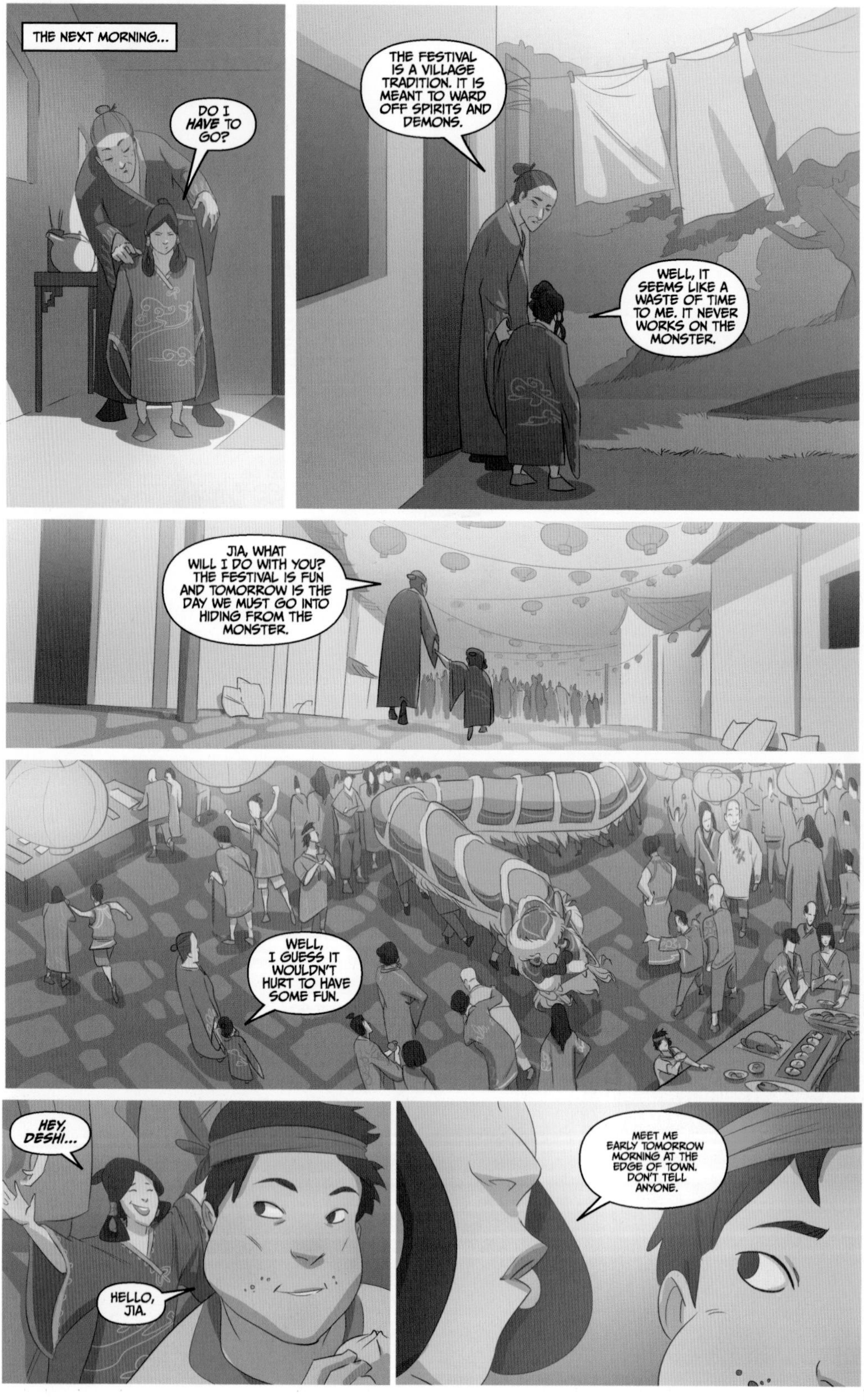
THE NEXT MORNING...
DO I HAVE TO GO?
THE FESTIVAL IS A VILLAGE TRADITION. IT IS MEANT TO WARD OFF SPIRITS AND DEMONS.
WELL, IT SEEMS LIKE A WASTE OF TIME TO ME. IT NEVER WORKS ON THE MONSTER.
JIA, WHAT WILL I DO WITH YOU? THE FESTIVAL IS FUN AND TOMORROW IS THE DAY WE MUST GO INTO HIDING FROM THE MONSTER.
WELL, I GUESS IT WOULDN'T HURT TO HAVE SOME FUN.
HEY, DESHI...
HELLO, JIA.
MEET ME EARLY TOMORROW MORNING AT THE EDGE OF TOWN. DON'T TELL ANYONE.

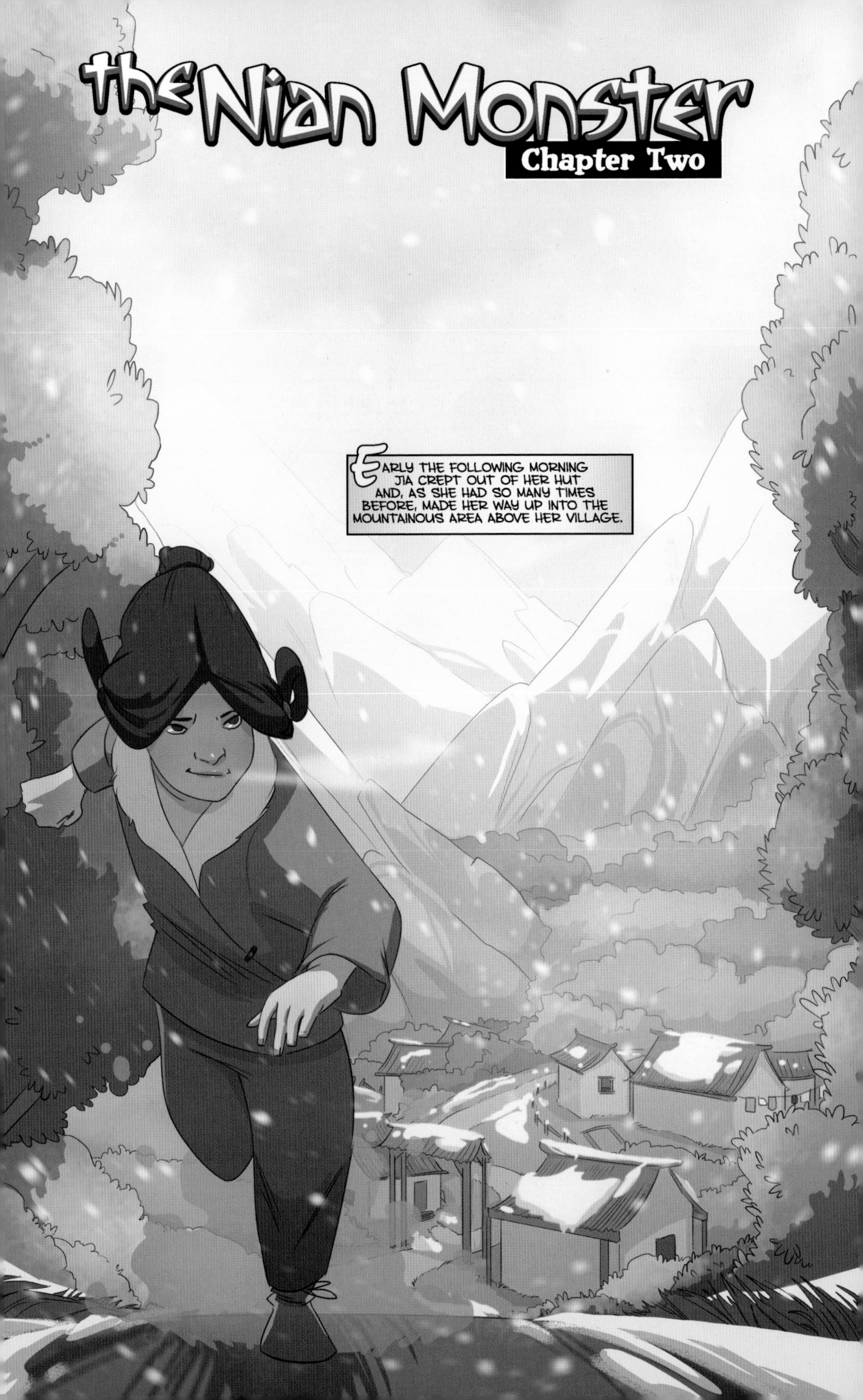
the Nian Monster
Chapter Two
EARLY THE FOLLOWING MORNING JIA CREPT OUT OF HER HUT AND, AS SHE HAD SO MANY TIMES BEFORE, MADE HER WAY UP INTO THE MOUNTAINOUS AREA ABOVE HER VILLAGE.

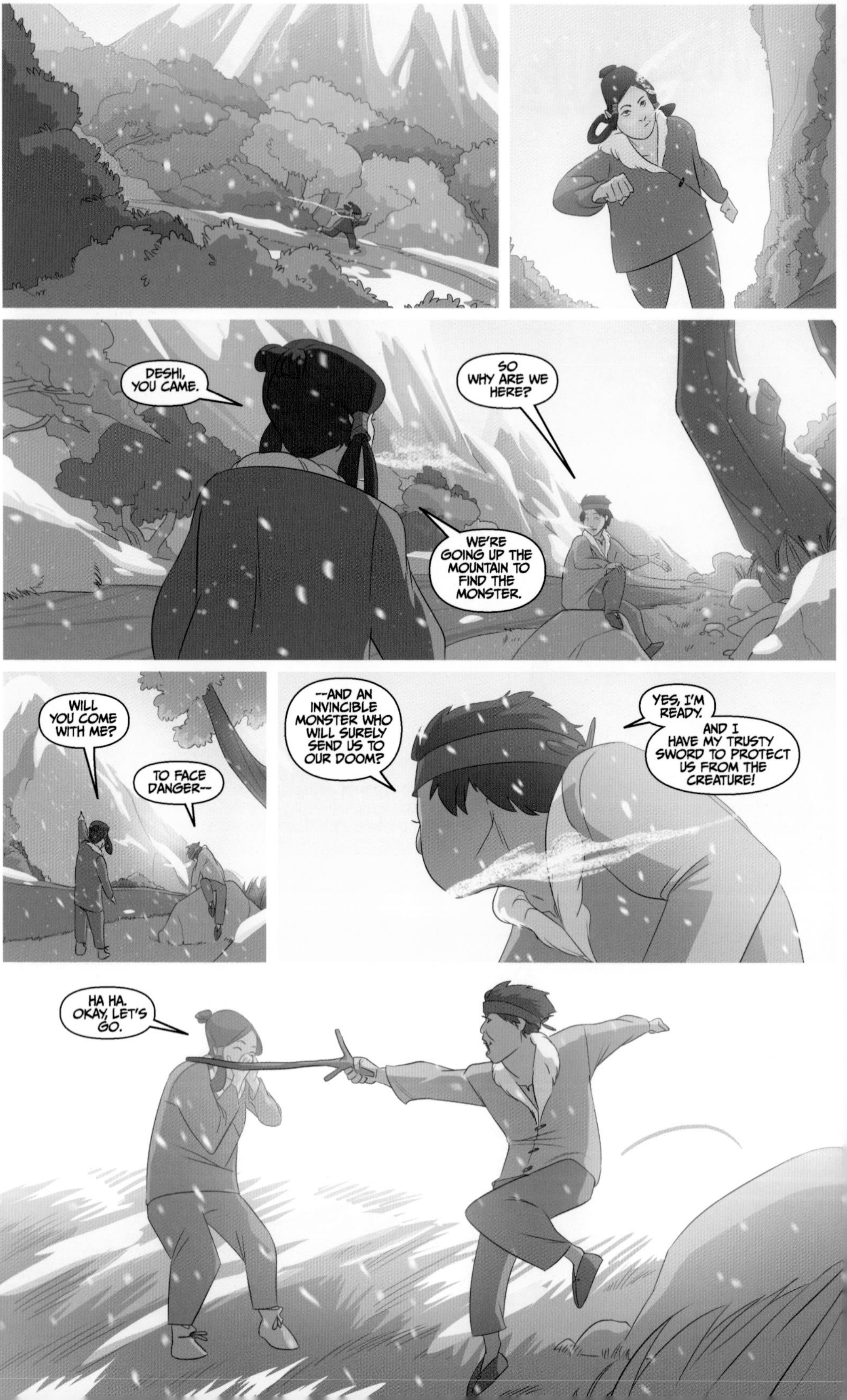
DESHI, YOU CAME.
SO WHY ARE WE HERE?
WE'RE GOING UP THE MOUNTAIN TO FIND THE MONSTER.
WILL YOU COME WITH ME?
TO FACE DANGER--
--AND AN INVINCIBLE MONSTER WHO WILL SURELY SEND US TO OUR DOOM?
YES, I'M READY.
AND I HAVE MY TRUSTY SWORD TO PROTECT US FROM THE CREATURE!
HA HA. OKAY, LET'S GO.

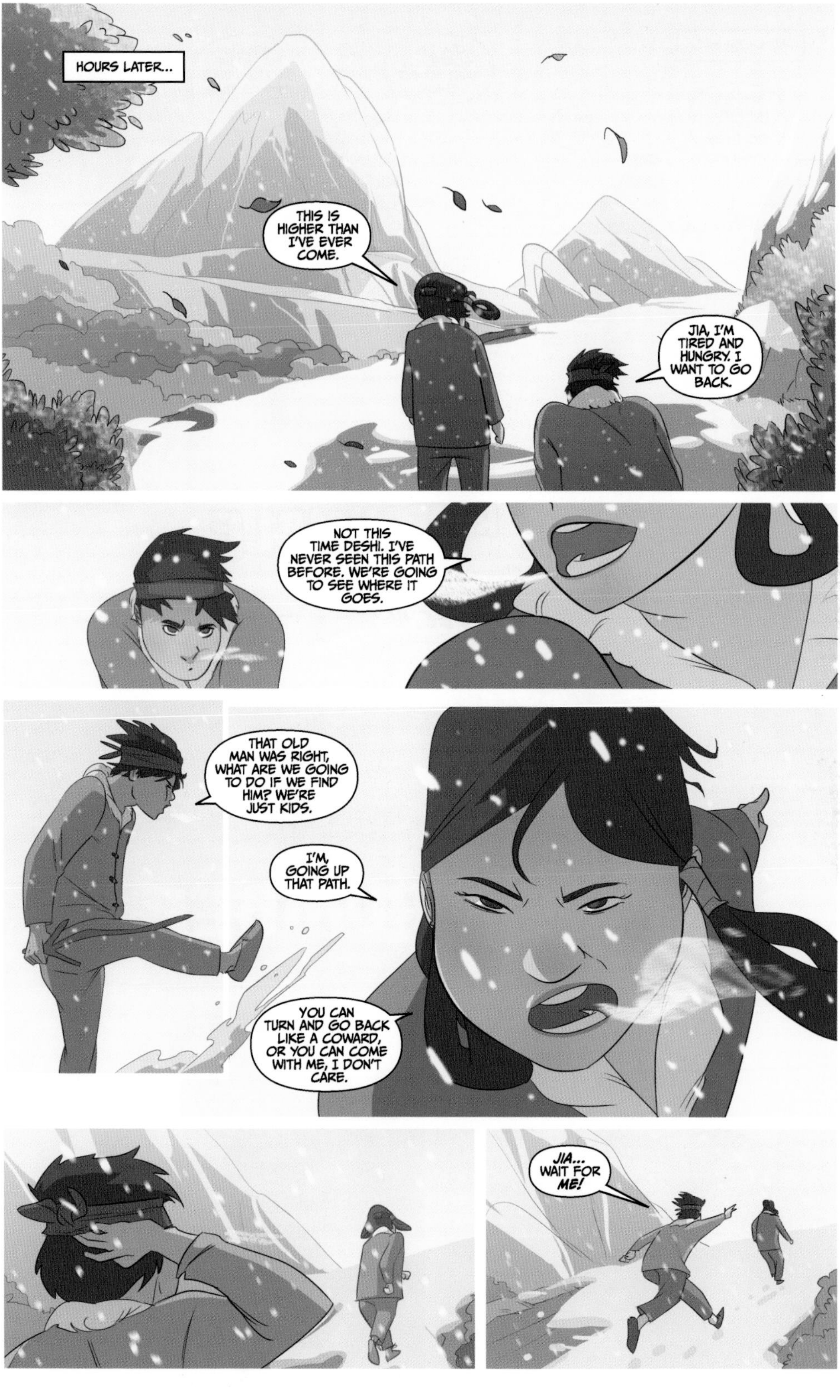
HOURS LATER...
THIS IS HIGHER THAN I'VE EVER COME.
JIA, I'M TIRED AND HUNGRY. I WANT TO GO BACK.
NOT THIS TIME DESHI. I'VE NEVER SEEN THIS PATH BEFORE. WE'RE GOING TO SEE WHERE IT GOES.
THAT OLD MAN WAS RIGHT, WHAT ARE WE GOING TO DO IF WE FIND HIM? WE'RE JUST KIDS.
I'M, GOING UP THAT PATH.
YOU CAN TURN AND GO BACK LIKE A COWARD, OR YOU CAN COME WITH ME, I DON'T CARE.
JIA... WAIT FOR ME!

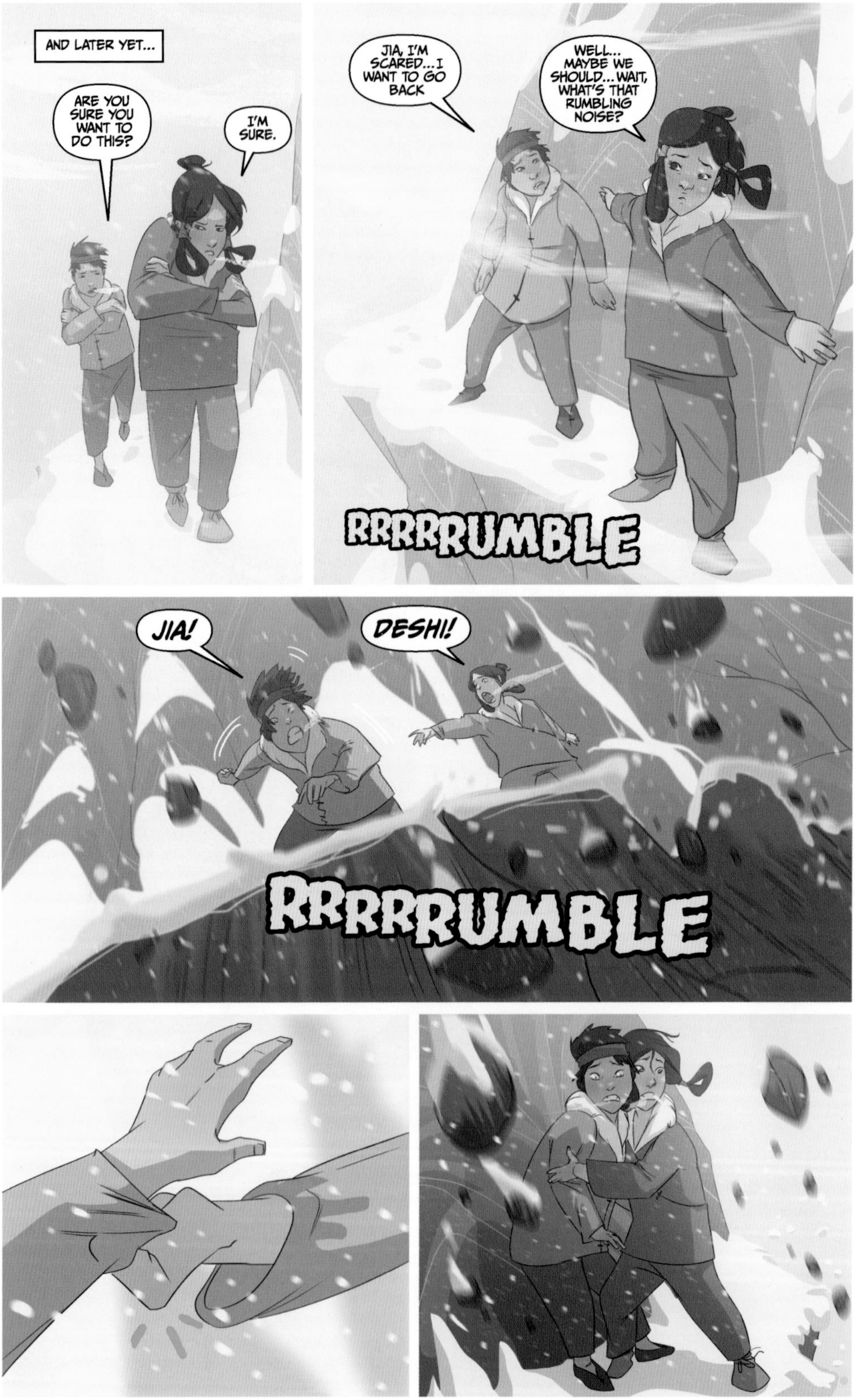
AND LATER YET...
ARE YOU SURE YOU WANT TO DO THIS?
I'M SURE.
JIA, I'M SCARED... I WANT TO GO BACK
WELL... MAYBE WE SHOULD... WAIT, WHAT'S THAT RUMBLING NOISE?
RRRRRUMBLE
JIA!
DESHI!
RRRRRUMBLE

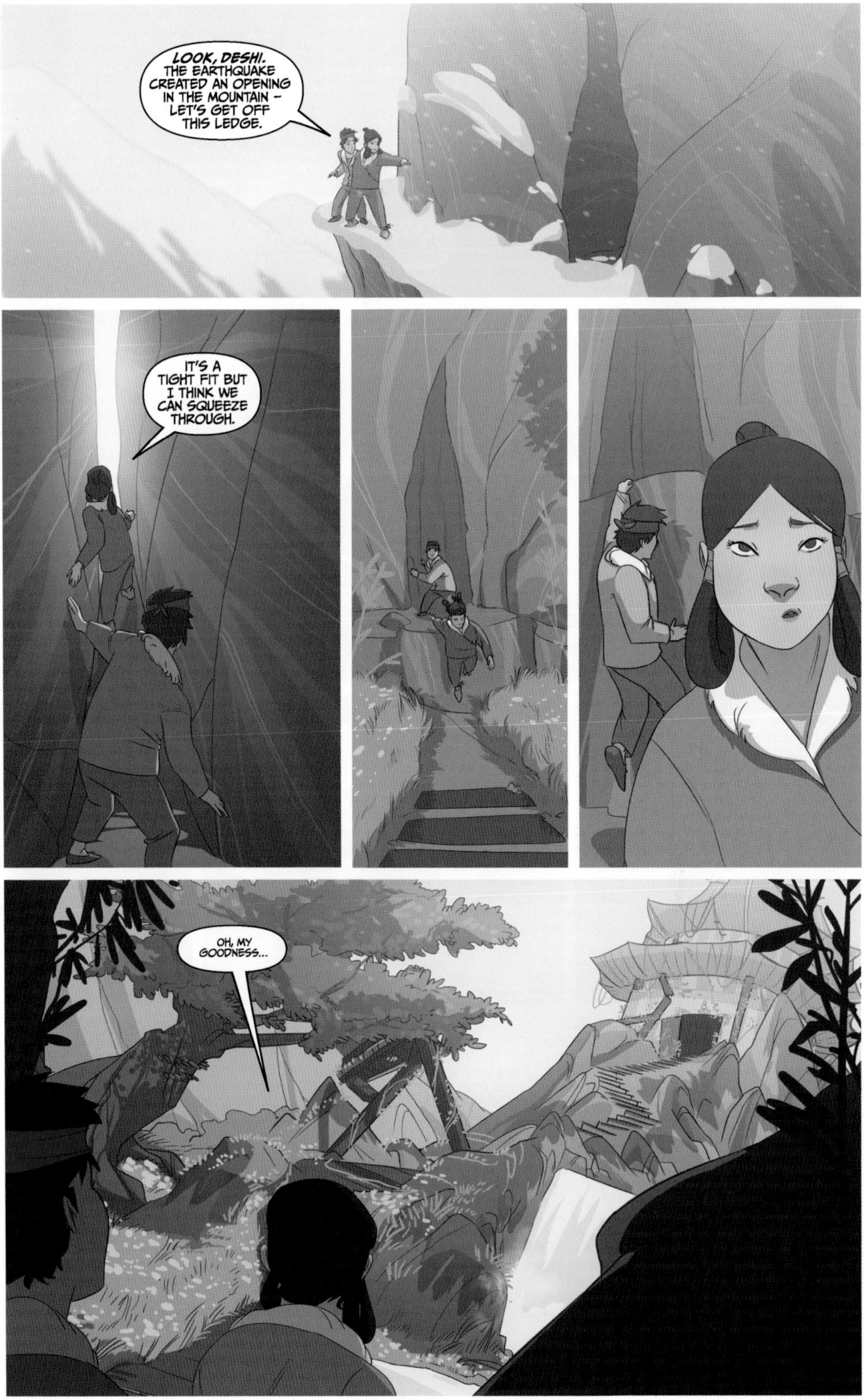
LOOK, DESHI. THE EARTHQUAKE CREATED AN OPENING IN THE MOUNTAIN – LET'S GET OFF THIS LEDGE.
IT'S A TIGHT FIT BUT I THINK WE CAN SQUEEZE THROUGH.
OH, MY GOODNESS...

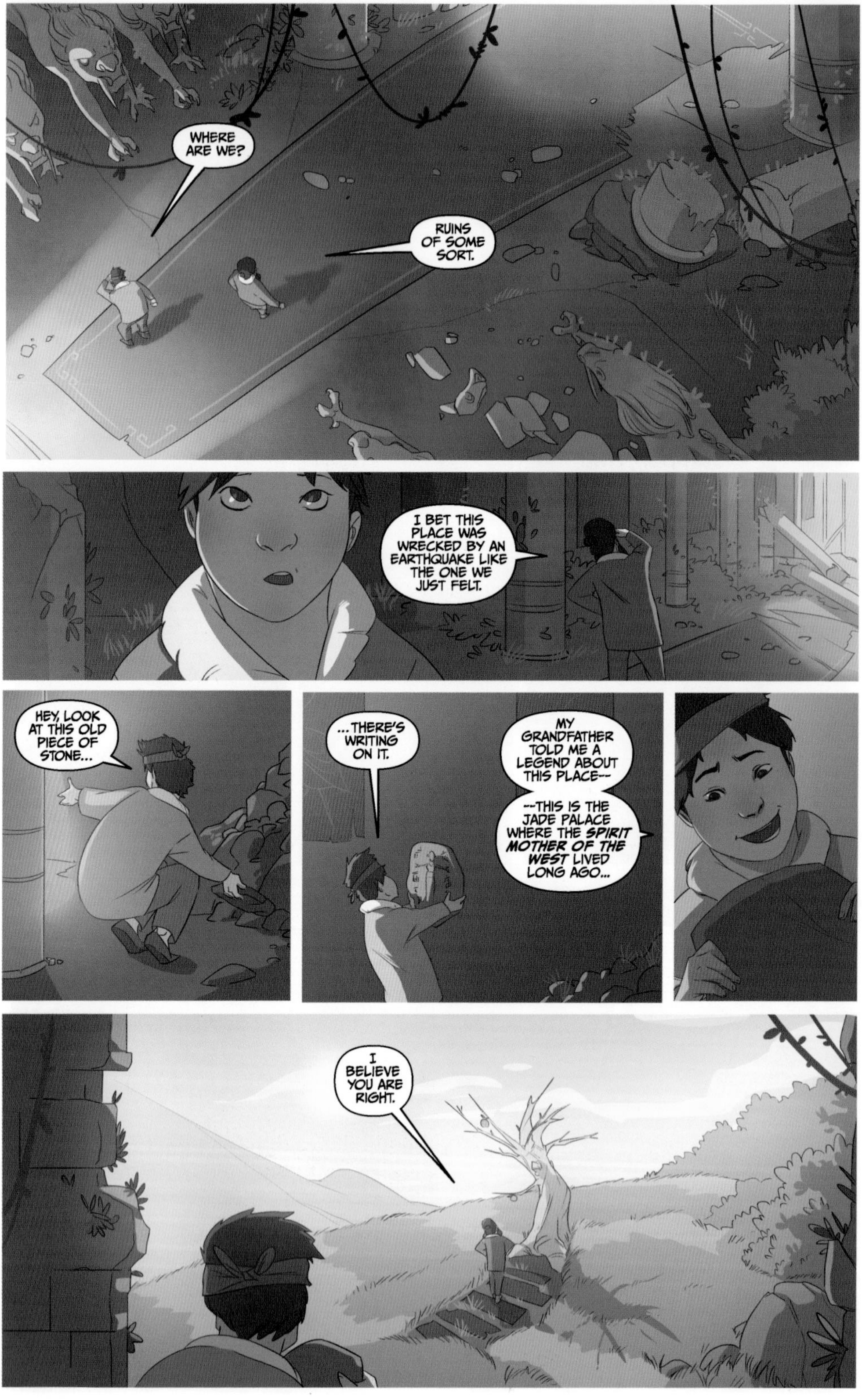
WHERE ARE WE?
RUINS OF SOME SORT.
I BET THIS PLACE WAS WRECKED BY AN EARTHQUAKE LIKE THE ONE WE JUST FELT.
HEY, LOOK AT THIS OLD PIECE OF STONE...
...THERE'S WRITING ON IT.
MY GRANDFATHER TOLD ME A LEGEND ABOUT THIS PLACE--
--THIS IS THE JADE PALACE WHERE THE *SPIRIT MOTHER OF THE WEST* LIVED LONG AGO...
I BELIEVE YOU ARE RIGHT.

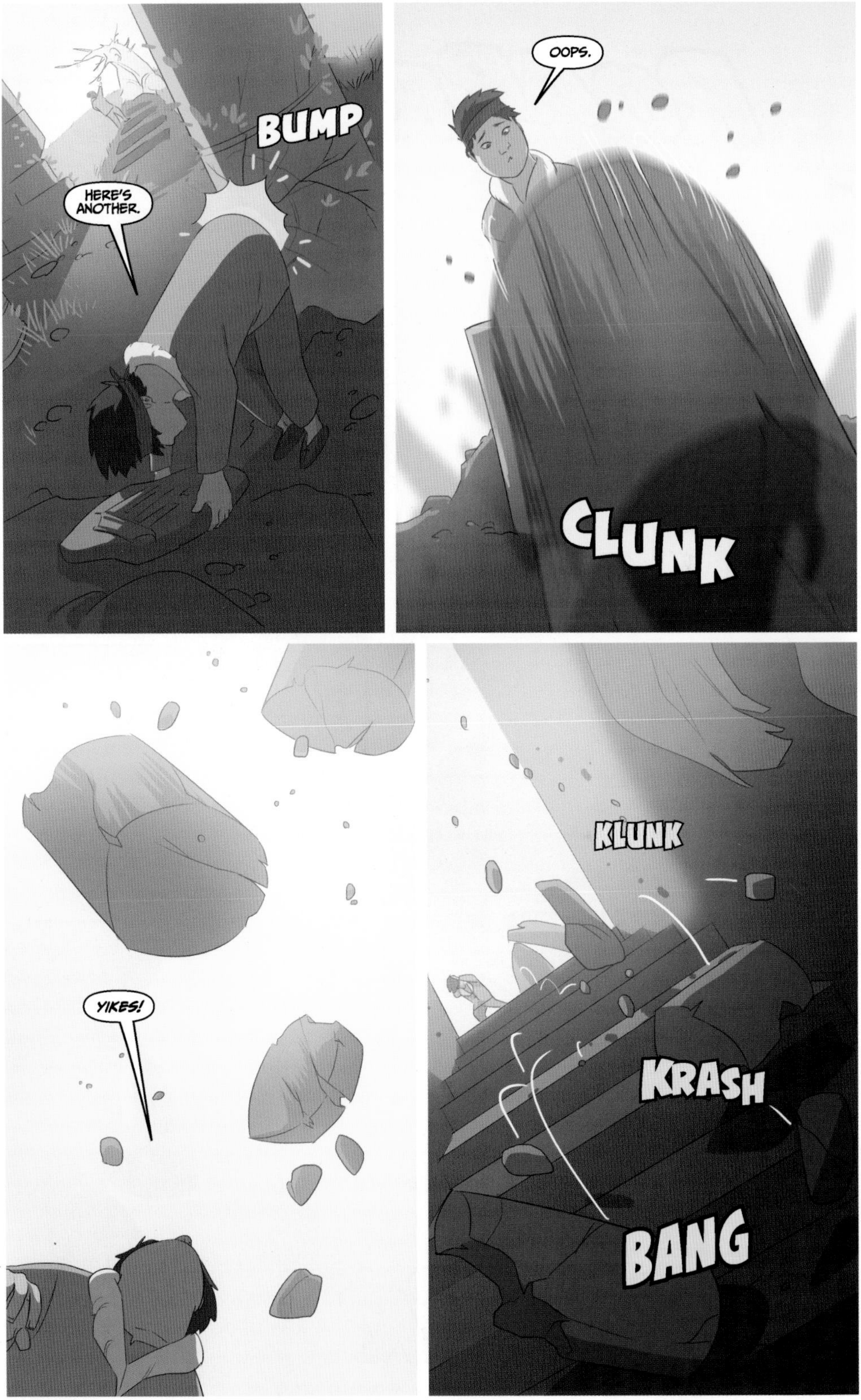
BUMP
HERE'S ANOTHER.
OOPS.
CLUNK
YIKES!
KLUNK
KRASH
BANG

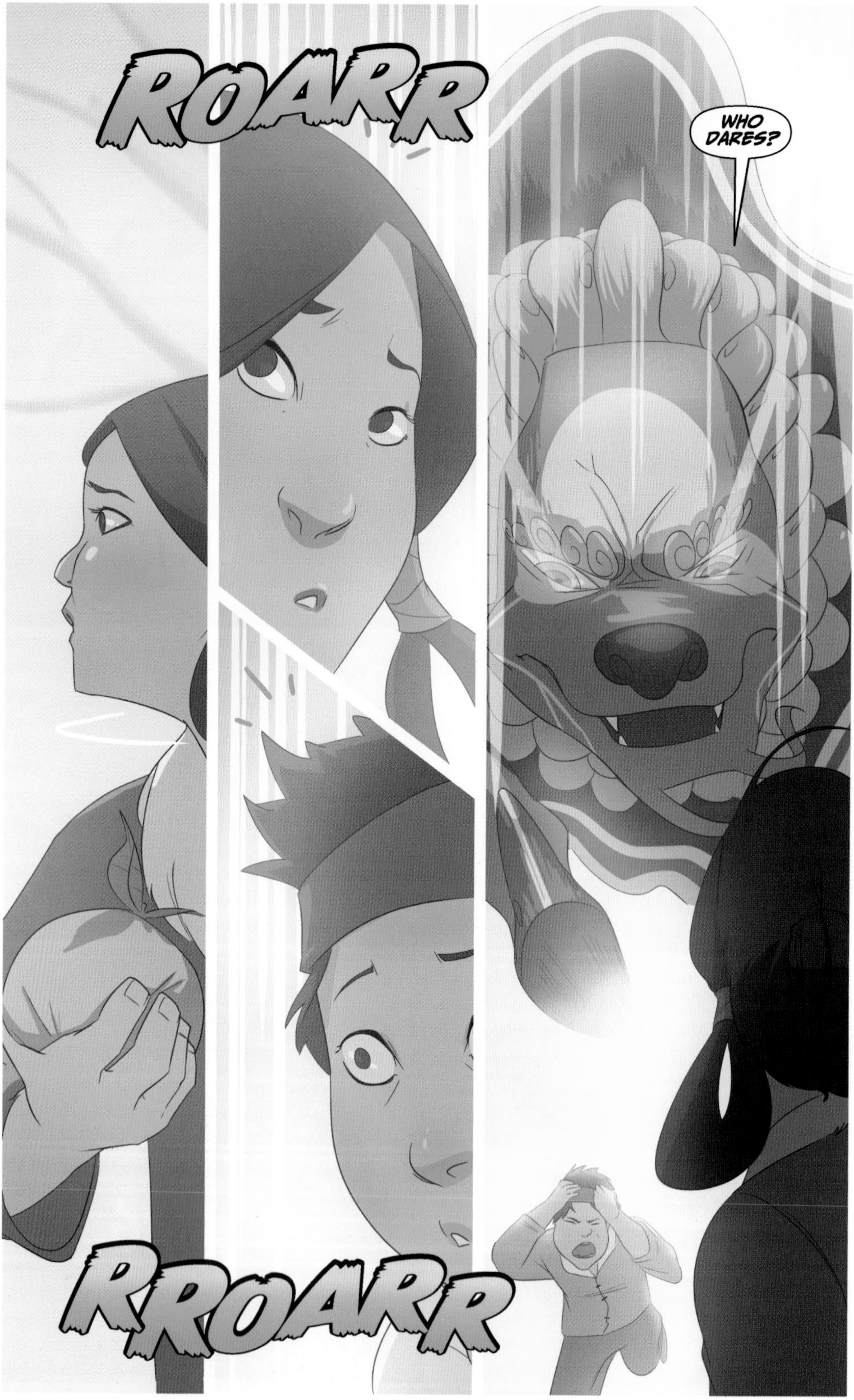
ROARR
WHO DARES?
RROARR

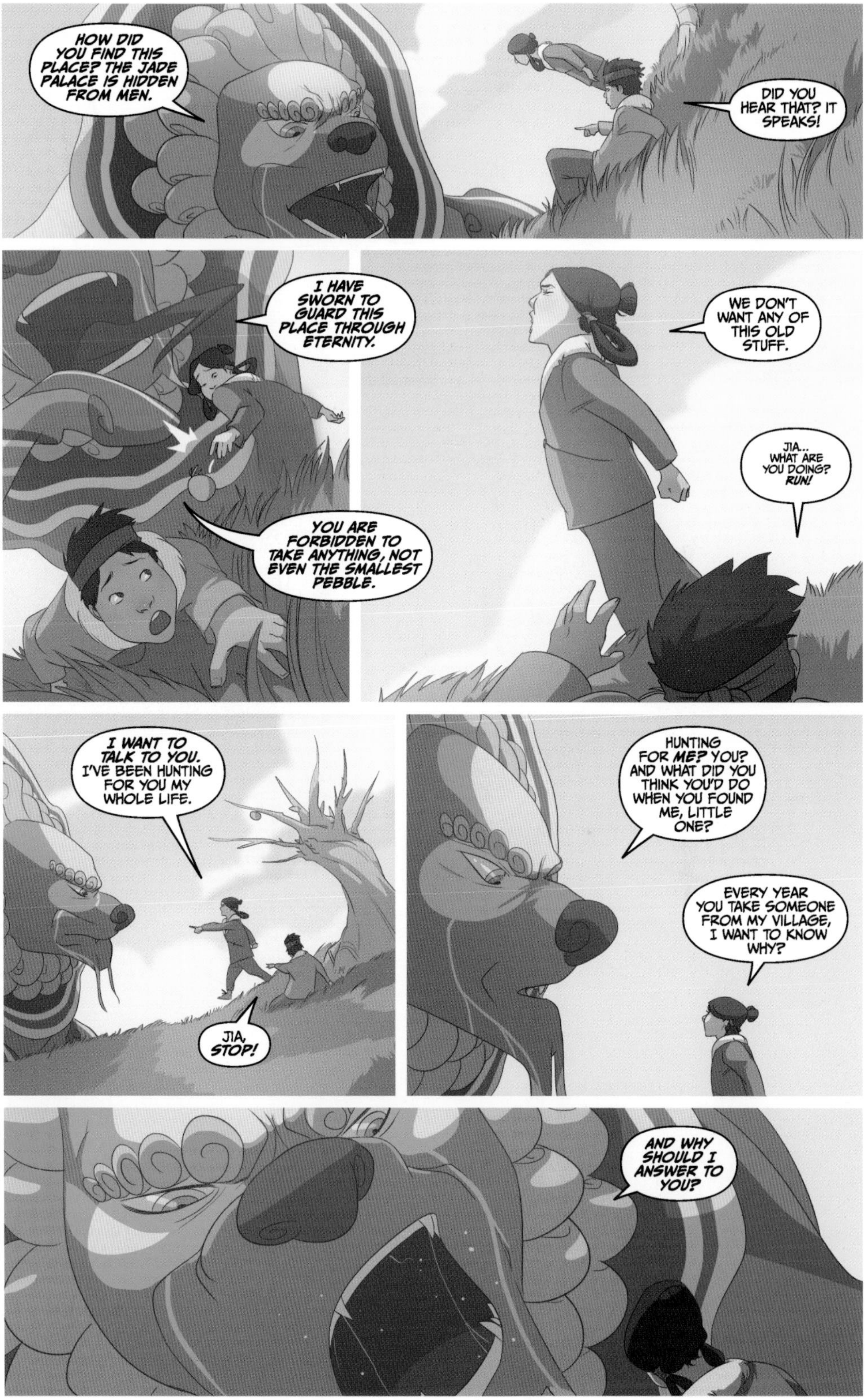
HOW DID YOU FIND THIS PLACE? THE JADE PALACE IS HIDDEN FROM MEN.
DID YOU HEAR THAT? IT SPEAKS!
I HAVE SWORN TO GUARD THIS PLACE THROUGH ETERNITY.
YOU ARE FORBIDDEN TO TAKE ANYTHING, NOT EVEN THE SMALLEST PEBBLE.
WE DON'T WANT ANY OF THIS OLD STUFF.
JIA... WHAT ARE YOU DOING? RUN!
I WANT TO TALK TO YOU. I'VE BEEN HUNTING FOR YOU MY WHOLE LIFE.
JIA, STOP!
HUNTING FOR ME? YOU? AND WHAT DID YOU THINK YOU'D DO WHEN YOU FOUND ME, LITTLE ONE?
EVERY YEAR YOU TAKE SOMEONE FROM MY VILLAGE, I WANT TO KNOW WHY?
AND WHY SHOULD I ANSWER TO YOU?

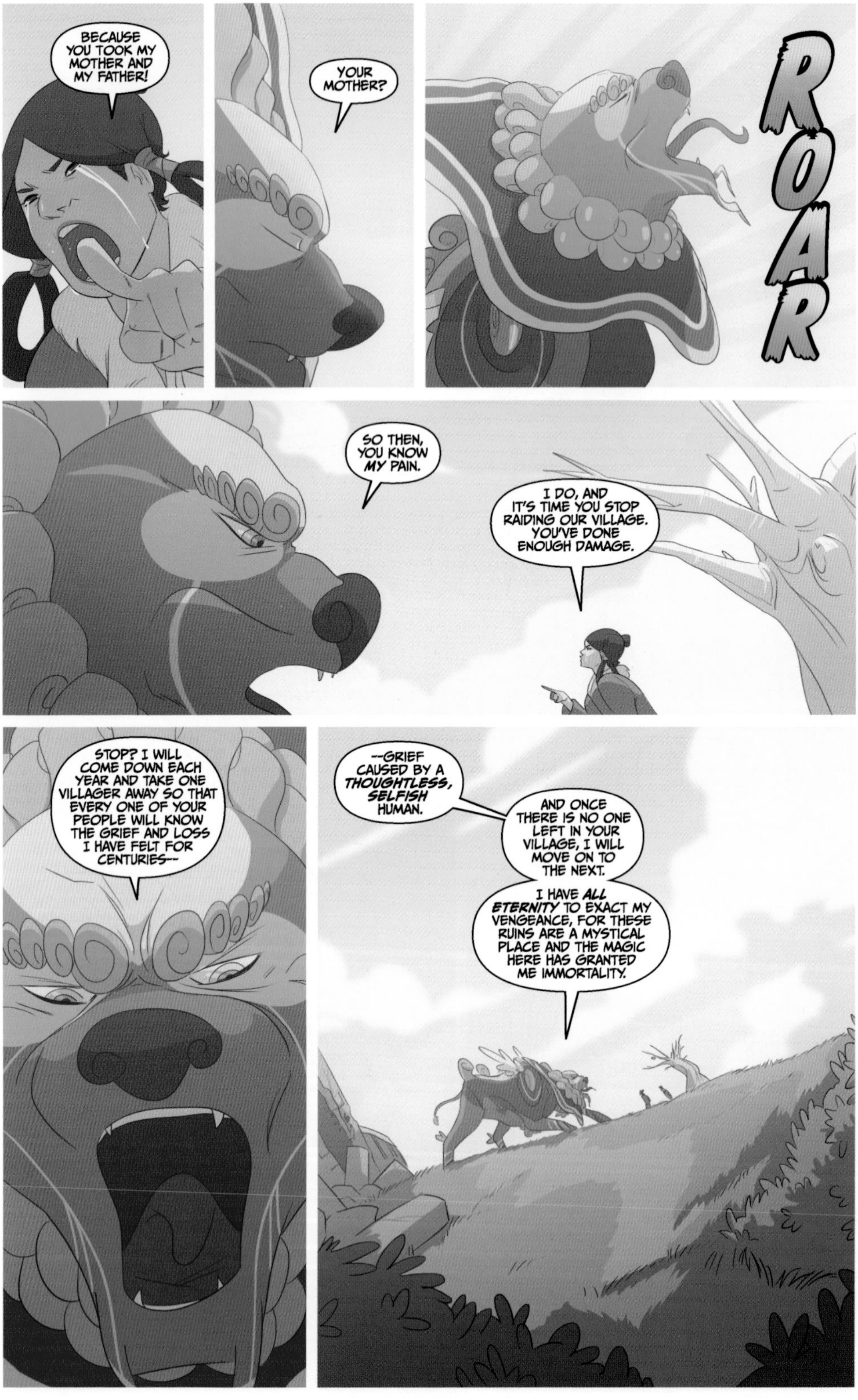
BECAUSE YOU TOOK MY MOTHER AND MY FATHER!
YOUR MOTHER?
ROAR
SO THEN, YOU KNOW MY PAIN.
I DO, AND IT'S TIME YOU STOP RAIDING OUR VILLAGE. YOU'VE DONE ENOUGH DAMAGE.
STOP? I WILL COME DOWN EACH YEAR AND TAKE ONE VILLAGER AWAY SO THAT EVERY ONE OF YOUR PEOPLE WILL KNOW THE GRIEF AND LOSS I HAVE FELT FOR CENTURIES--
--GRIEF CAUSED BY A THOUGHTLESS, SELFISH HUMAN.
AND ONCE THERE IS NO ONE LEFT IN YOUR VILLAGE, I WILL MOVE ON TO THE NEXT.
I HAVE ALL ETERNITY TO EXACT MY VENGEANCE, FOR THESE RUINS ARE A MYSTICAL PLACE AND THE MAGIC HERE HAS GRANTED ME IMMORTALITY.

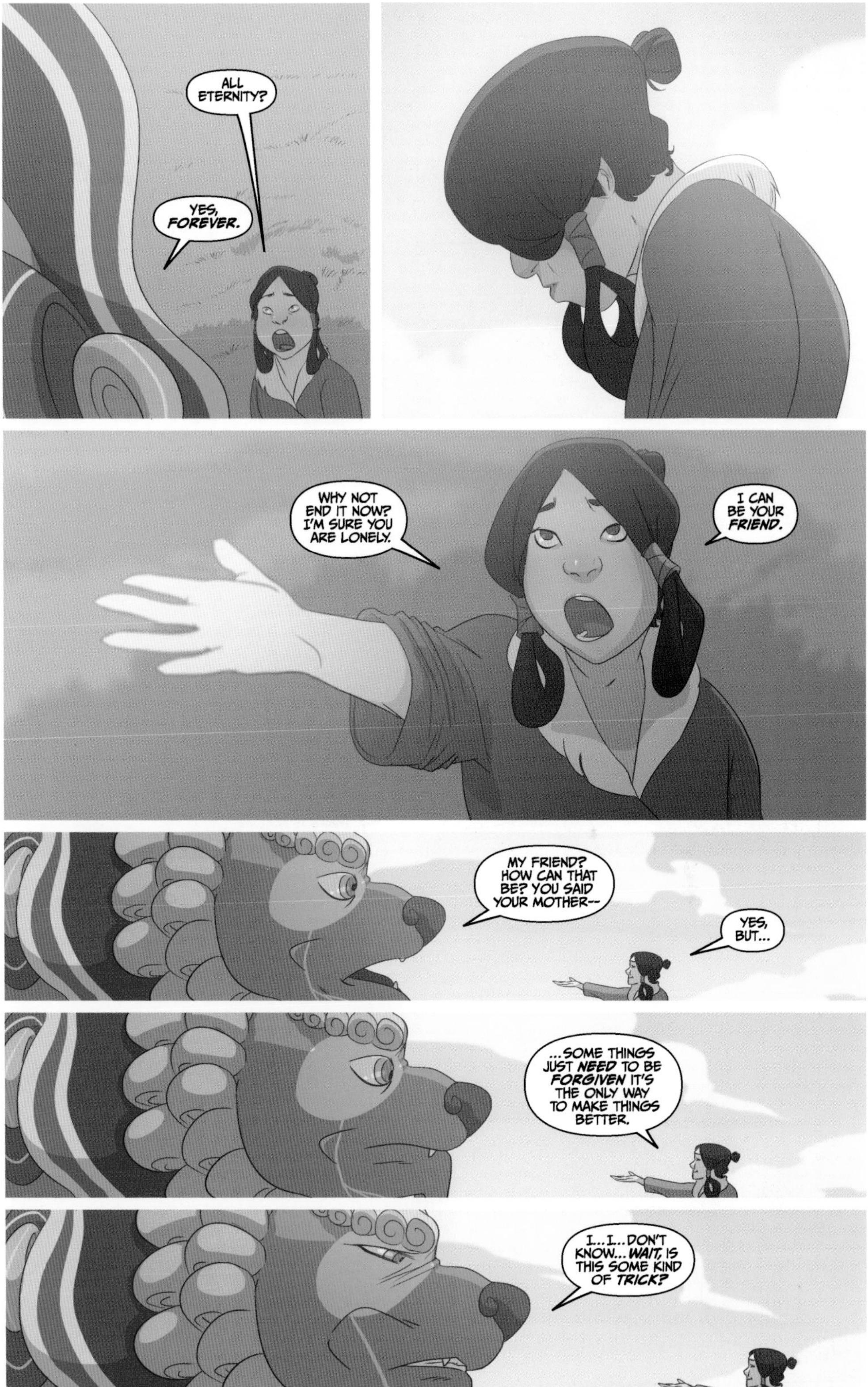
ALL ETERNITY?
YES, FOREVER.
WHY NOT END IT NOW? I'M SURE YOU ARE LONELY.
I CAN BE YOUR FRIEND.
MY FRIEND? HOW CAN THAT BE? YOU SAID YOUR MOTHER--
YES, BUT...
...SOME THINGS JUST NEED TO BE FORGIVEN IT'S THE ONLY WAY TO MAKE THINGS BETTER.
I...I...DON'T KNOW...WAIT, IS THIS SOME KIND OF TRICK?

ROOAR

I'LL TELL YOU WHAT I'VE DECIDED...

...I'LL *EAT* THE TWO OF YOU *BEFORE* MY ANNUAL VISIT TO YOUR VILLAGE.

OH NO YOU WON'T.

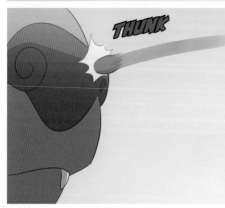

THUNK

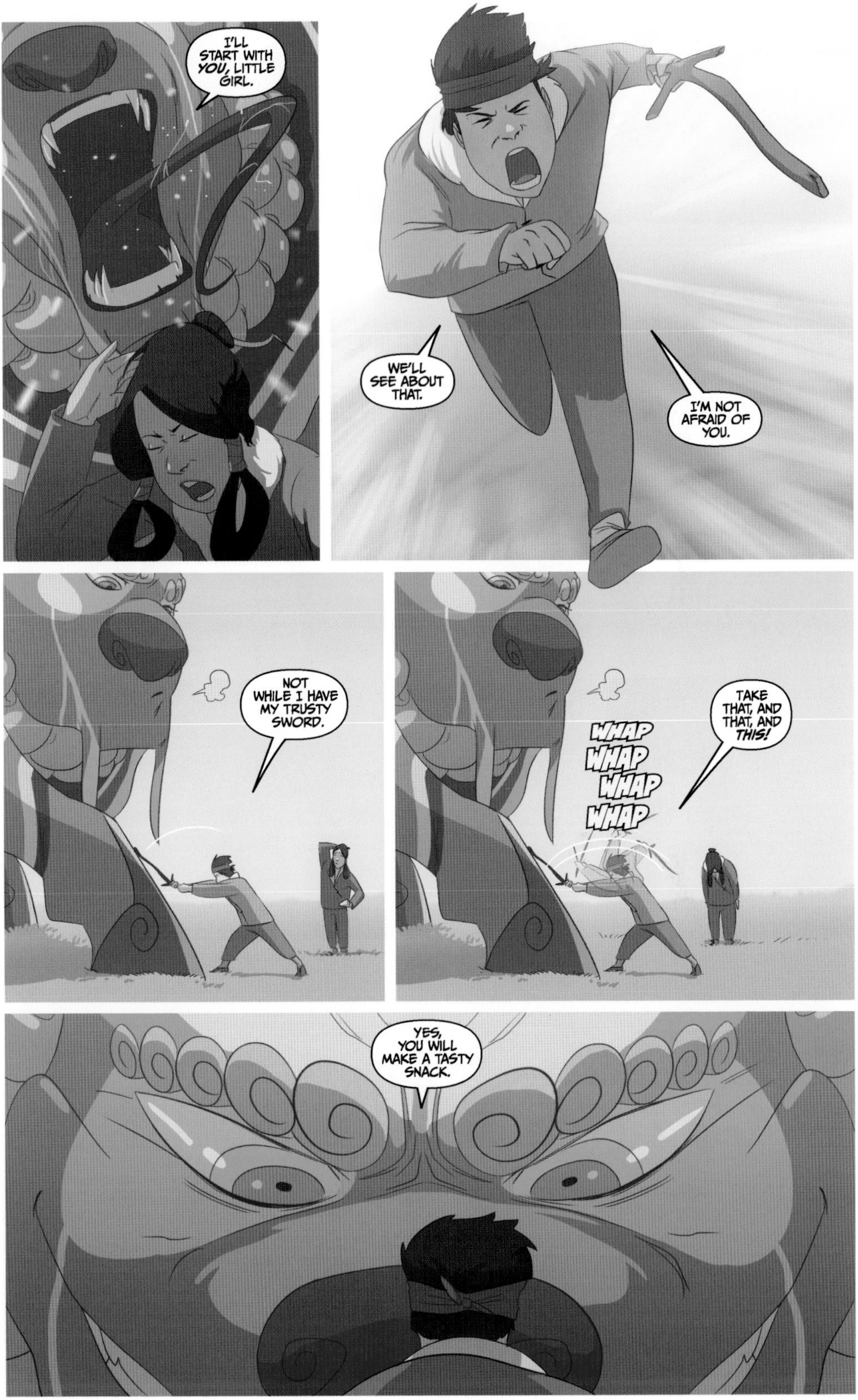
I'LL START WITH YOU, LITTLE GIRL.
WE'LL SEE ABOUT THAT.
I'M NOT AFRAID OF YOU.
NOT WHILE I HAVE MY TRUSTY SWORD.
WHAP
WHAP
WHAP
WHAP
TAKE THAT, AND THAT, AND THIS!
YES, YOU WILL MAKE A TASTY SNACK.

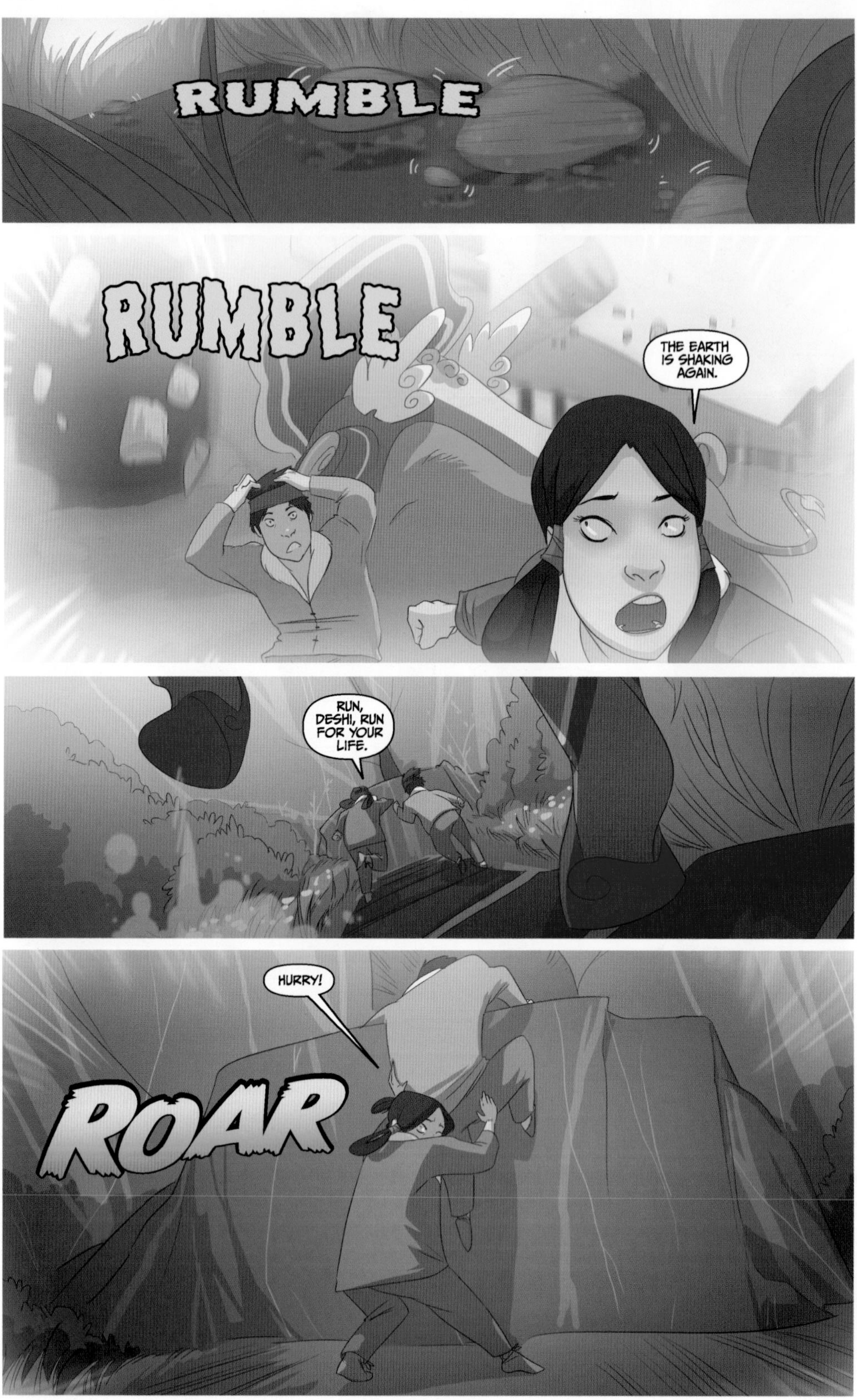
RUMBLE
RUMBLE
THE EARTH IS SHAKING AGAIN.
RUN, DESHI, RUN FOR YOUR LIFE.
HURRY!
ROAR

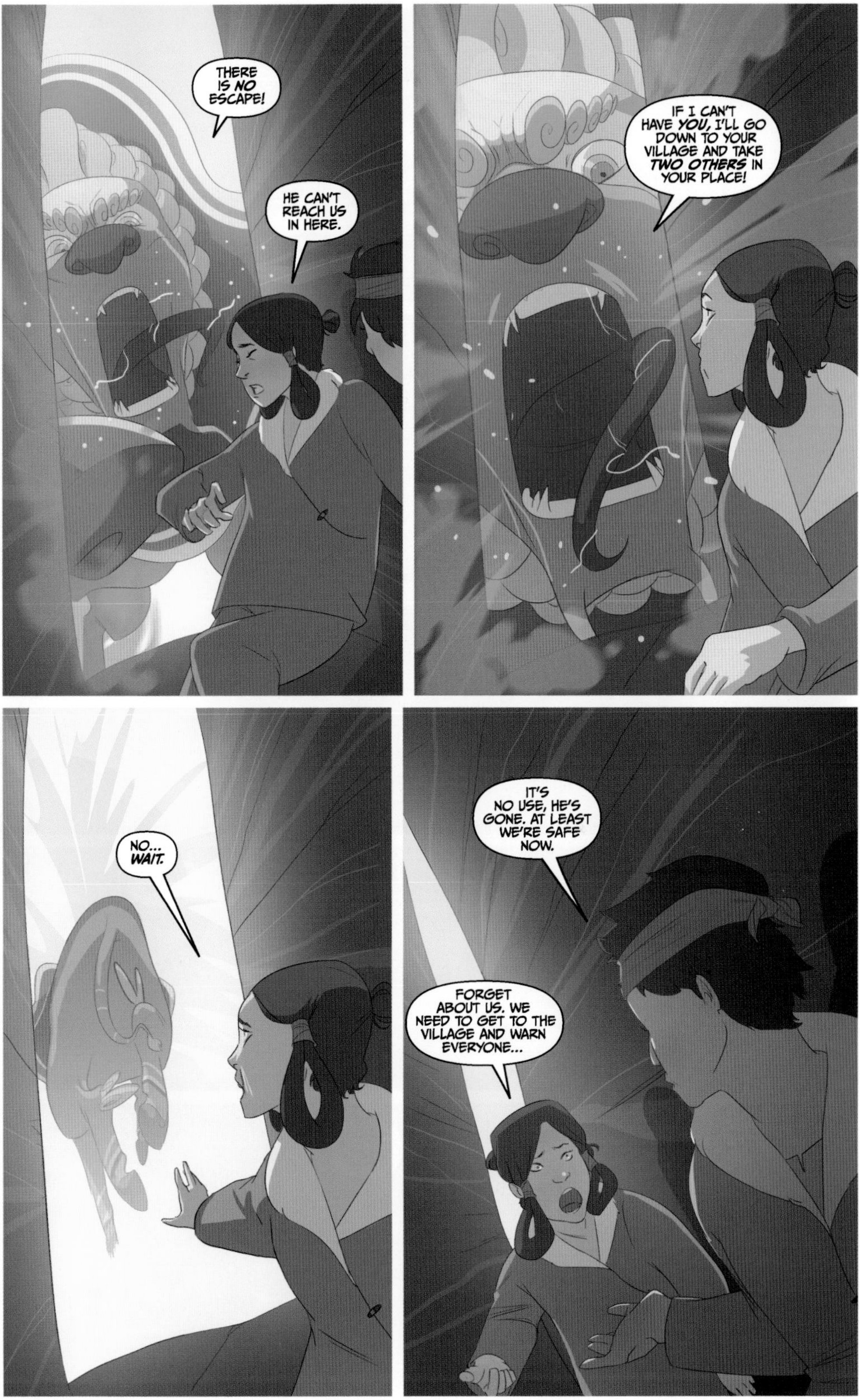
THERE IS *NO* ESCAPE!
HE CAN'T REACH US IN HERE.
IF I CAN'T HAVE *YOU*, I'LL GO DOWN TO YOUR VILLAGE AND TAKE *TWO OTHERS* IN YOUR PLACE!
NO... *WAIT.*
IT'S NO USE, HE'S GONE. AT LEAST WE'RE SAFE NOW.
FORGET ABOUT US. WE NEED TO GET TO THE VILLAGE AND WARN EVERYONE...

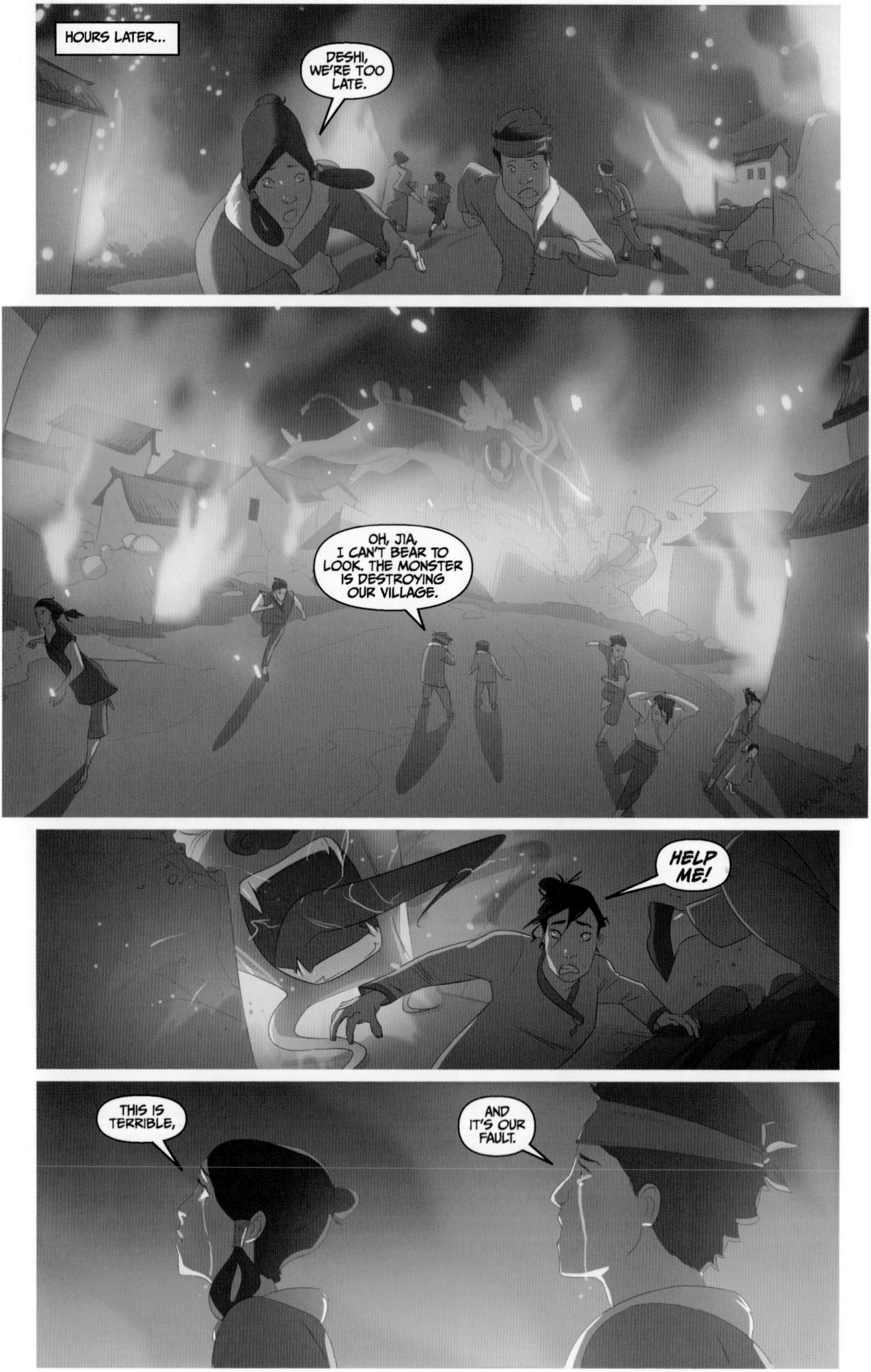
HOURS LATER...
DESHI, WE'RE TOO LATE.
OH, JIA, I CAN'T BEAR TO LOOK. THE MONSTER IS DESTROYING OUR VILLAGE.
HELP ME!
THIS IS TERRIBLE,
AND IT'S OUR FAULT.

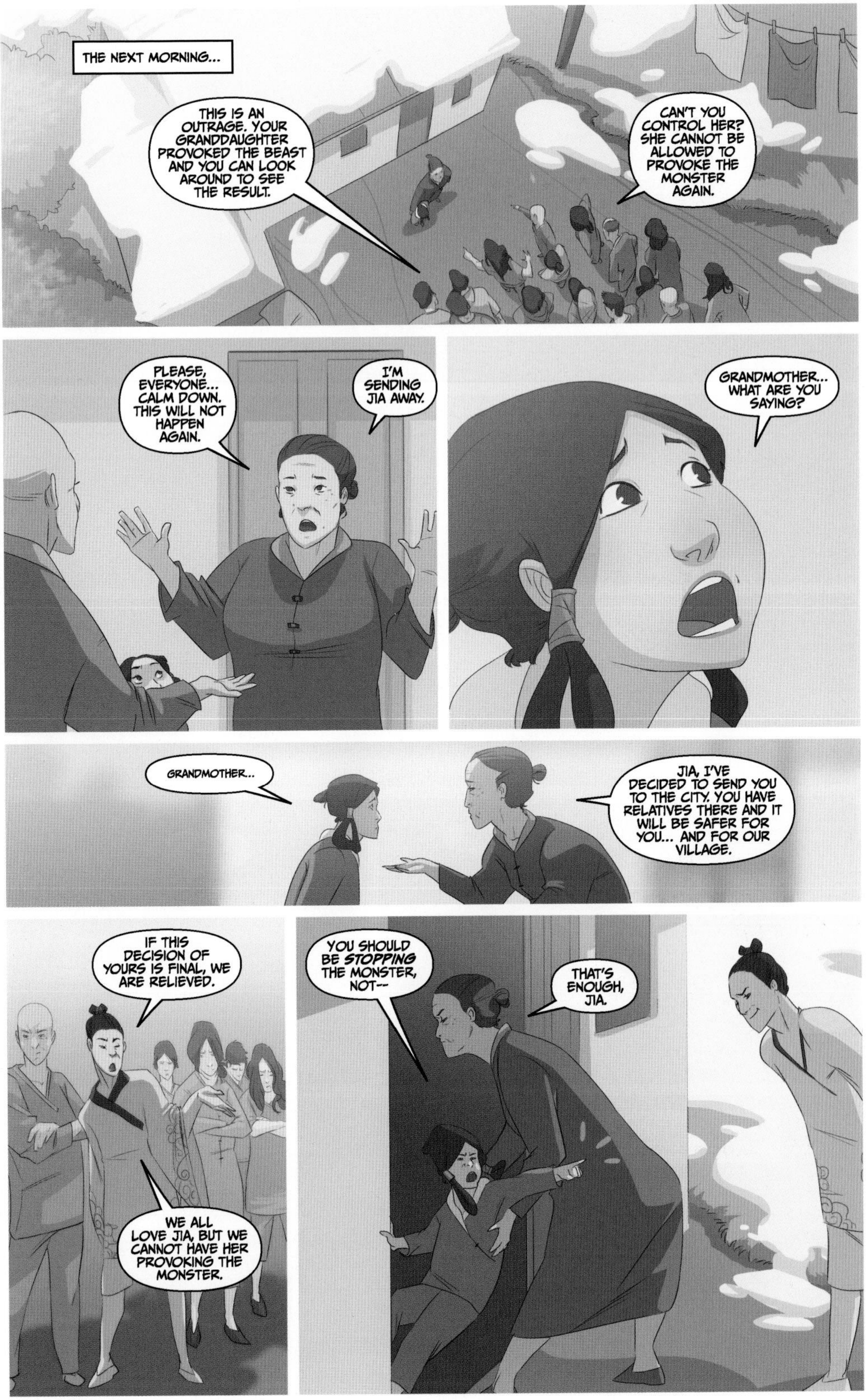
THE NEXT MORNING...
THIS IS AN OUTRAGE. YOUR GRANDDAUGHTER PROVOKED THE BEAST AND YOU CAN LOOK AROUND TO SEE THE RESULT.
CAN'T YOU CONTROL HER? SHE CANNOT BE ALLOWED TO PROVOKE THE MONSTER AGAIN.
PLEASE, EVERYONE... CALM DOWN. THIS WILL NOT HAPPEN AGAIN.
I'M SENDING JIA AWAY.
GRANDMOTHER... WHAT ARE YOU SAYING?
GRANDMOTHER...
JIA, I'VE DECIDED TO SEND YOU TO THE CITY. YOU HAVE RELATIVES THERE AND IT WILL BE SAFER FOR YOU... AND FOR OUR VILLAGE.
IF THIS DECISION OF YOURS IS FINAL, WE ARE RELIEVED.
WE ALL LOVE JIA, BUT WE CANNOT HAVE HER PROVOKING THE MONSTER.
YOU SHOULD BE STOPPING THE MONSTER, NOT--
THAT'S ENOUGH, JIA.

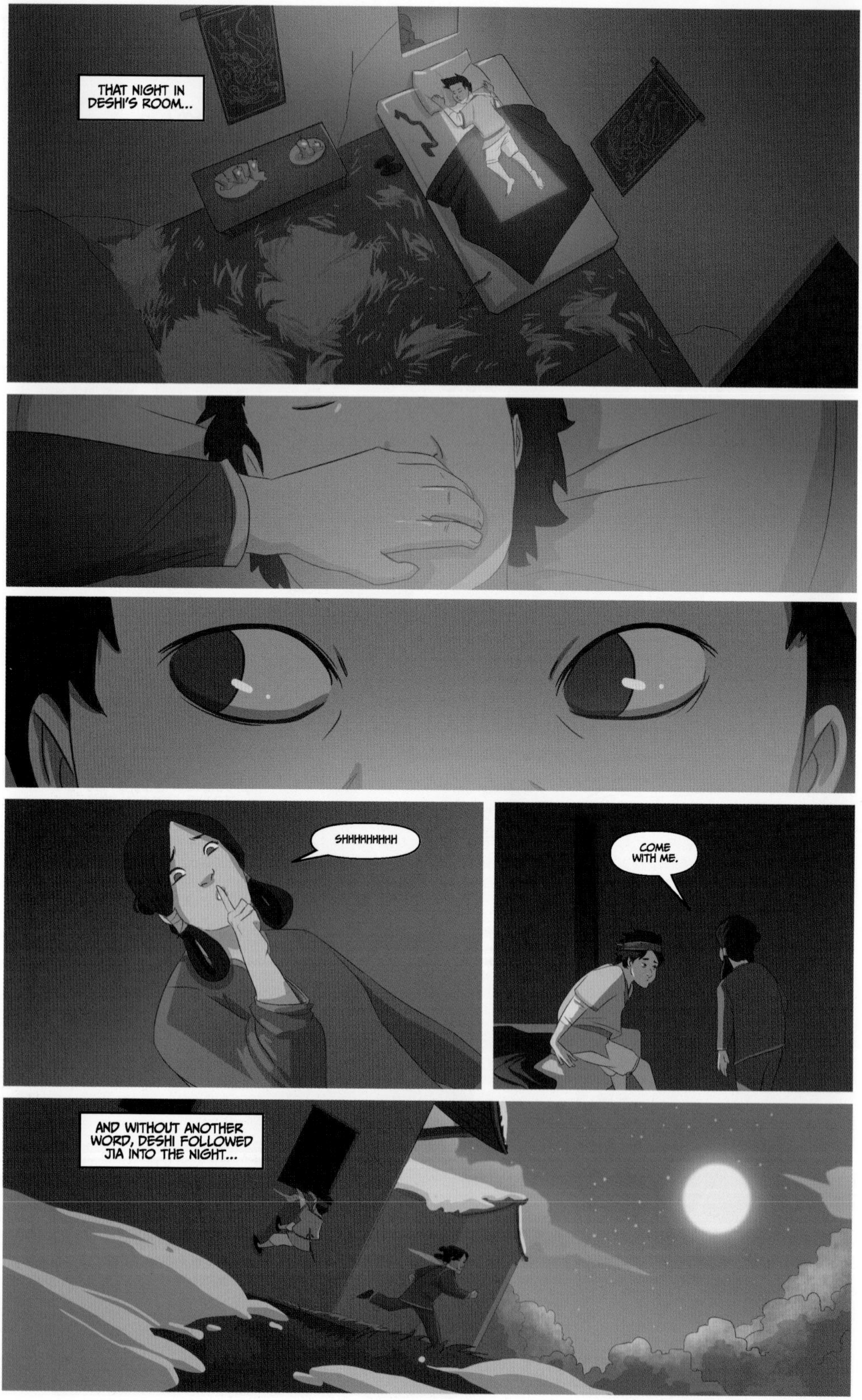
THAT NIGHT IN DESHI'S ROOM...
SHHHHHHHHH
COME WITH ME.
AND WITHOUT ANOTHER WORD, DESHI FOLLOWED JIA INTO THE NIGHT...

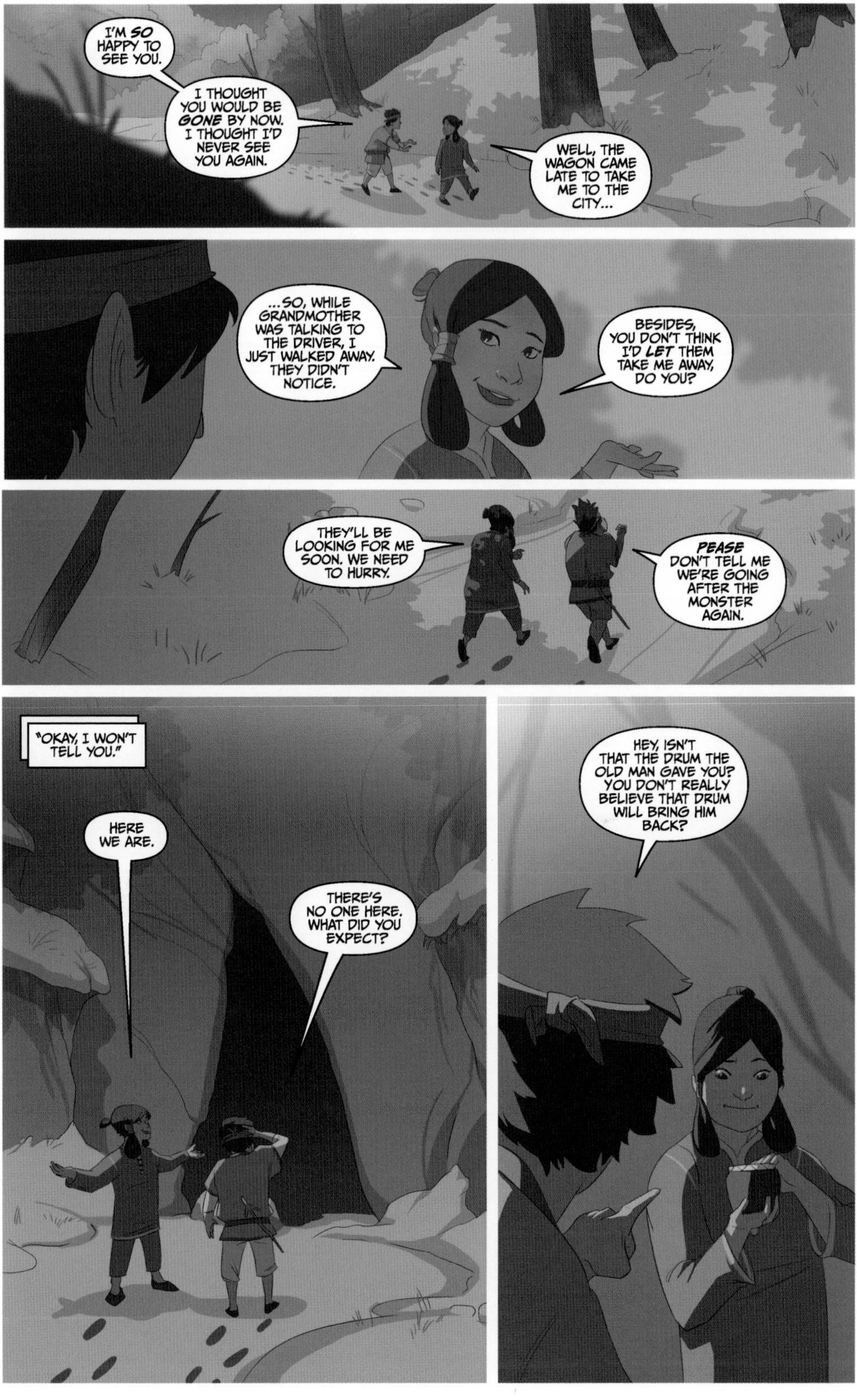
I'M SO HAPPY TO SEE YOU.
I THOUGHT YOU WOULD BE GONE BY NOW. I THOUGHT I'D NEVER SEE YOU AGAIN.
WELL, THE WAGON CAME LATE TO TAKE ME TO THE CITY...
...SO, WHILE GRANDMOTHER WAS TALKING TO THE DRIVER, I JUST WALKED AWAY. THEY DIDN'T NOTICE.
BESIDES, YOU DON'T THINK I'D LET THEM TAKE ME AWAY, DO YOU?
THEY'LL BE LOOKING FOR ME SOON. WE NEED TO HURRY.
PEASE DON'T TELL ME WE'RE GOING AFTER THE MONSTER AGAIN.
"OKAY, I WON'T TELL YOU."
HERE WE ARE.
THERE'S NO ONE HERE. WHAT DID YOU EXPECT?
HEY, ISN'T THAT THE DRUM THE OLD MAN GAVE YOU? YOU DON'T REALLY BELIEVE THAT DRUM WILL BRING HIM BACK?

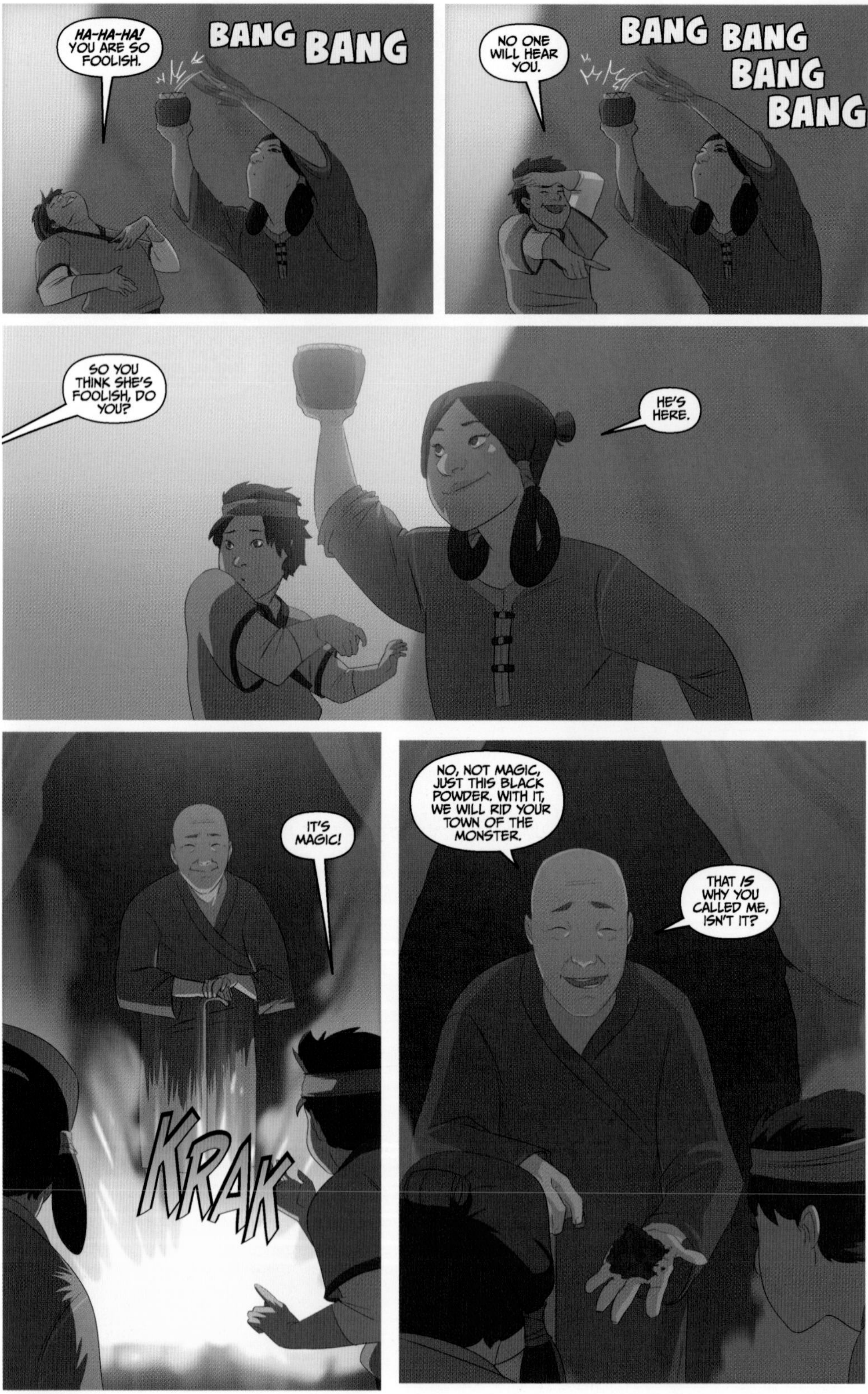
HA-HA-HA! YOU ARE SO FOOLISH.
BANG BANG
NO ONE WILL HEAR YOU.
BANG BANG BANG BANG
SO YOU THINK SHE'S FOOLISH, DO YOU?
HE'S HERE.
IT'S MAGIC!
KRAK
NO, NOT MAGIC, JUST THIS BLACK POWDER. WITH IT, WE WILL RID YOUR TOWN OF THE MONSTER.
THAT IS WHY YOU CALLED ME, ISN'T IT?

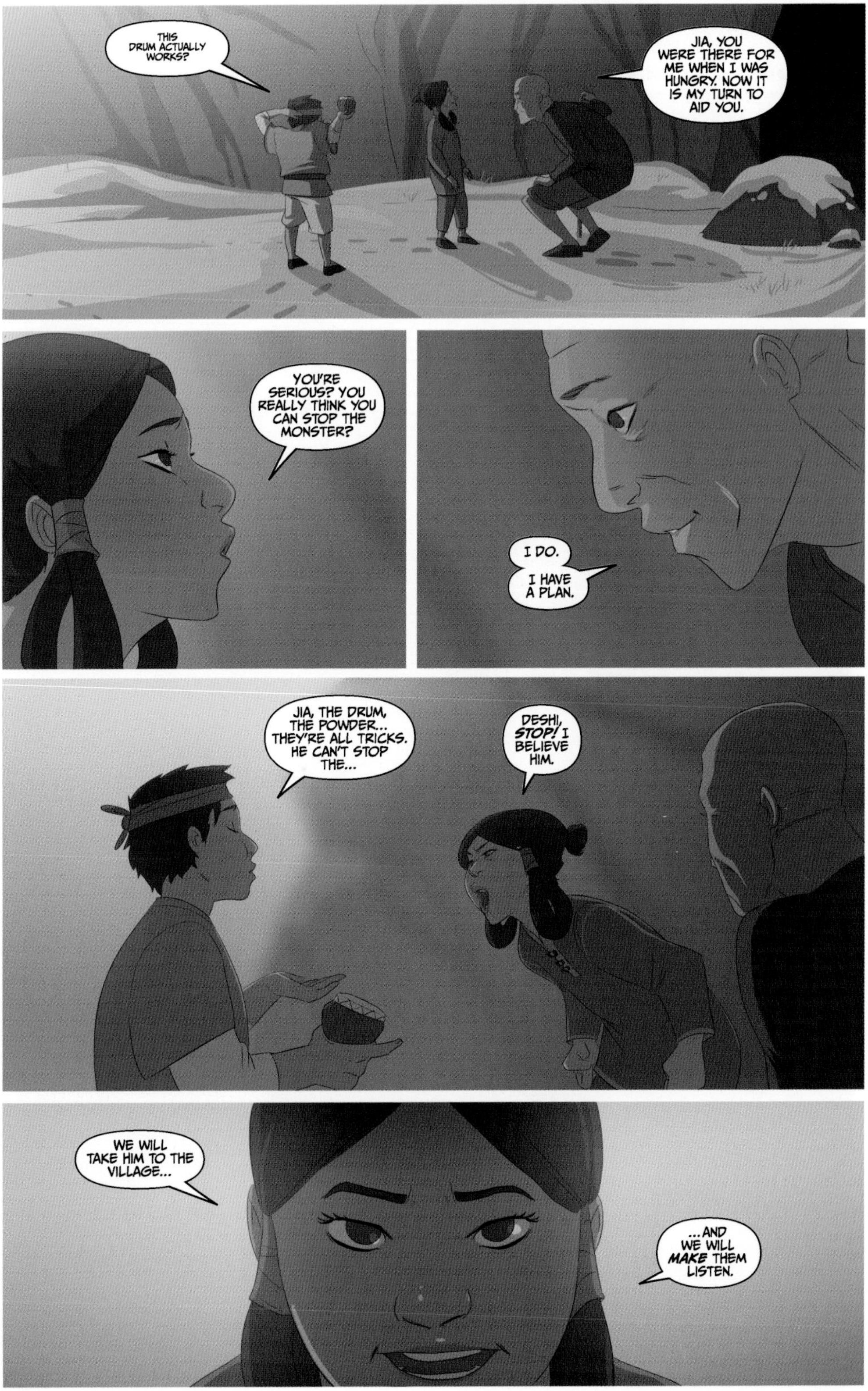
THIS DRUM ACTUALLY WORKS?
JIA, YOU WERE THERE FOR ME WHEN I WAS HUNGRY. NOW IT IS MY TURN TO AID YOU.
YOU'RE SERIOUS? YOU REALLY THINK YOU CAN STOP THE MONSTER?
I DO.
I HAVE A PLAN.
JIA, THE DRUM, THE POWDER... THEY'RE ALL TRICKS. HE CAN'T STOP THE...
DESHI, STOP! I BELIEVE HIM.
WE WILL TAKE HIM TO THE VILLAGE...
...AND WE WILL MAKE THEM LISTEN.

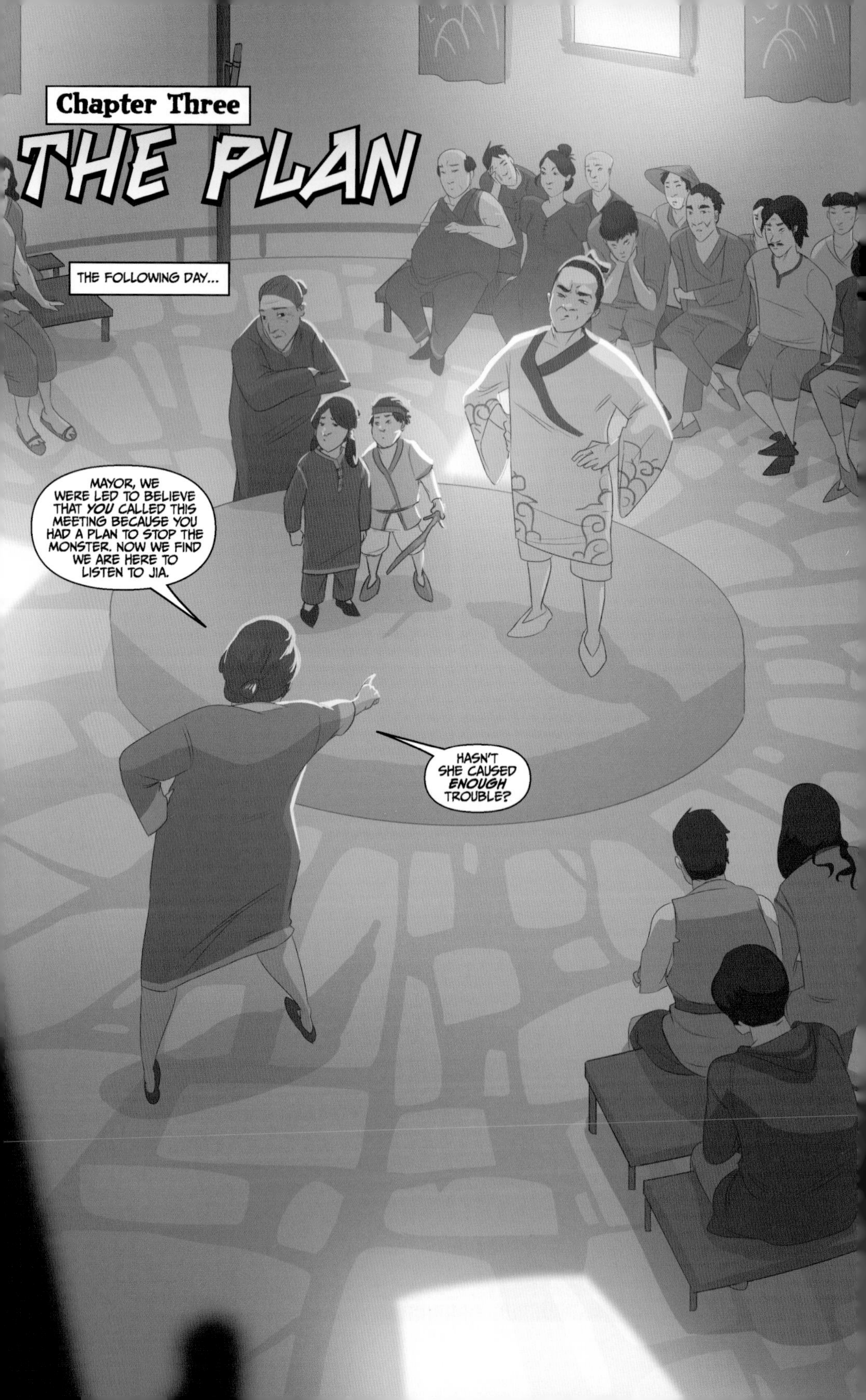

Chapter Three
THE PLAN
THE FOLLOWING DAY...
MAYOR, WE WERE LED TO BELIEVE THAT YOU CALLED THIS MEETING BECAUSE YOU HAD A PLAN TO STOP THE MONSTER. NOW WE FIND WE ARE HERE TO LISTEN TO JIA.
HASN'T SHE CAUSED ENOUGH TROUBLE?

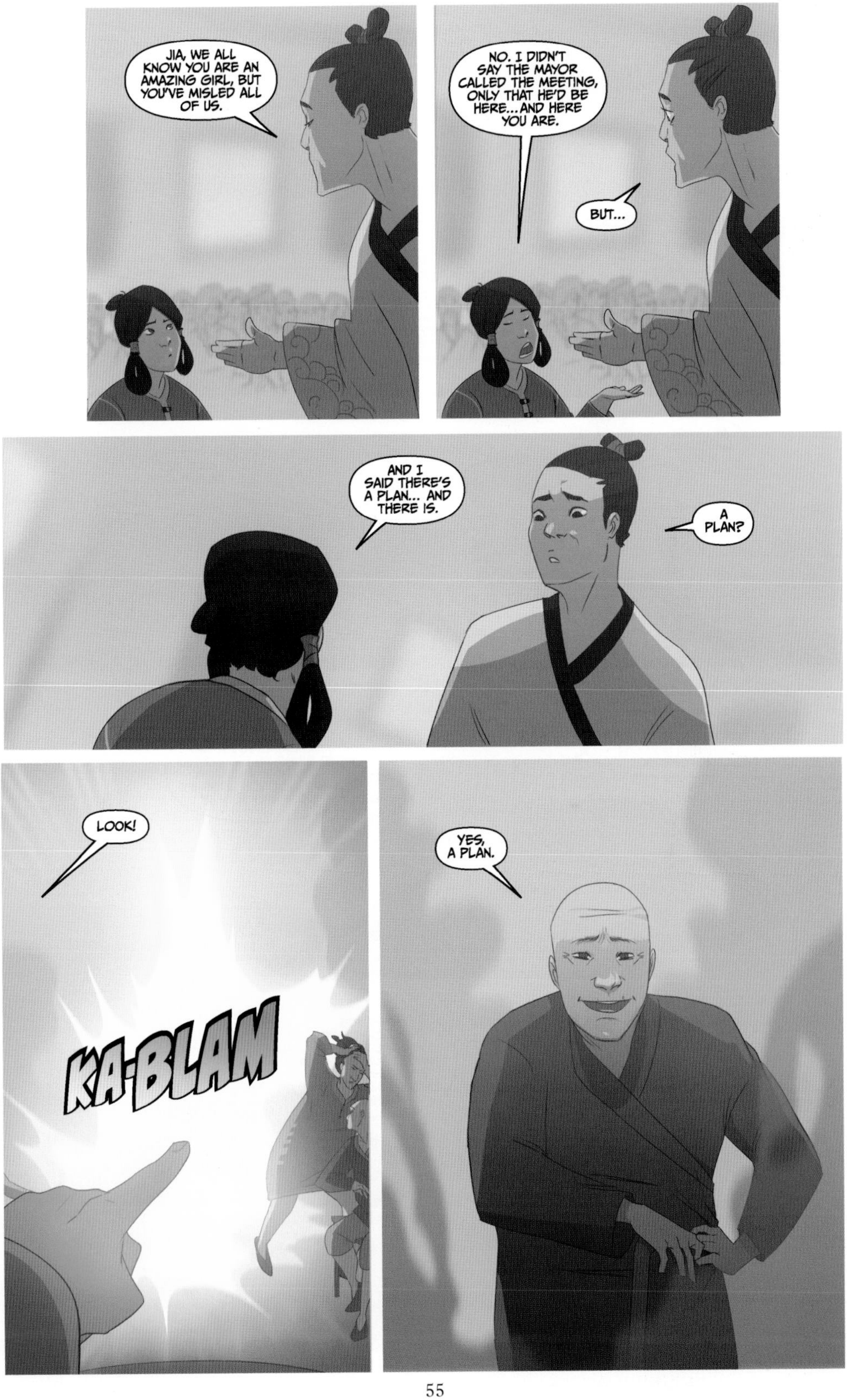
JIA, WE ALL KNOW YOU ARE AN AMAZING GIRL, BUT YOU'VE MISLED ALL OF US.
NO. I DIDN'T SAY THE MAYOR CALLED THE MEETING, ONLY THAT HE'D BE HERE... AND HERE YOU ARE.
BUT...
AND I SAID THERE'S A PLAN... AND THERE IS.
A PLAN?
LOOK!
KA-BLAM
YES, A PLAN.

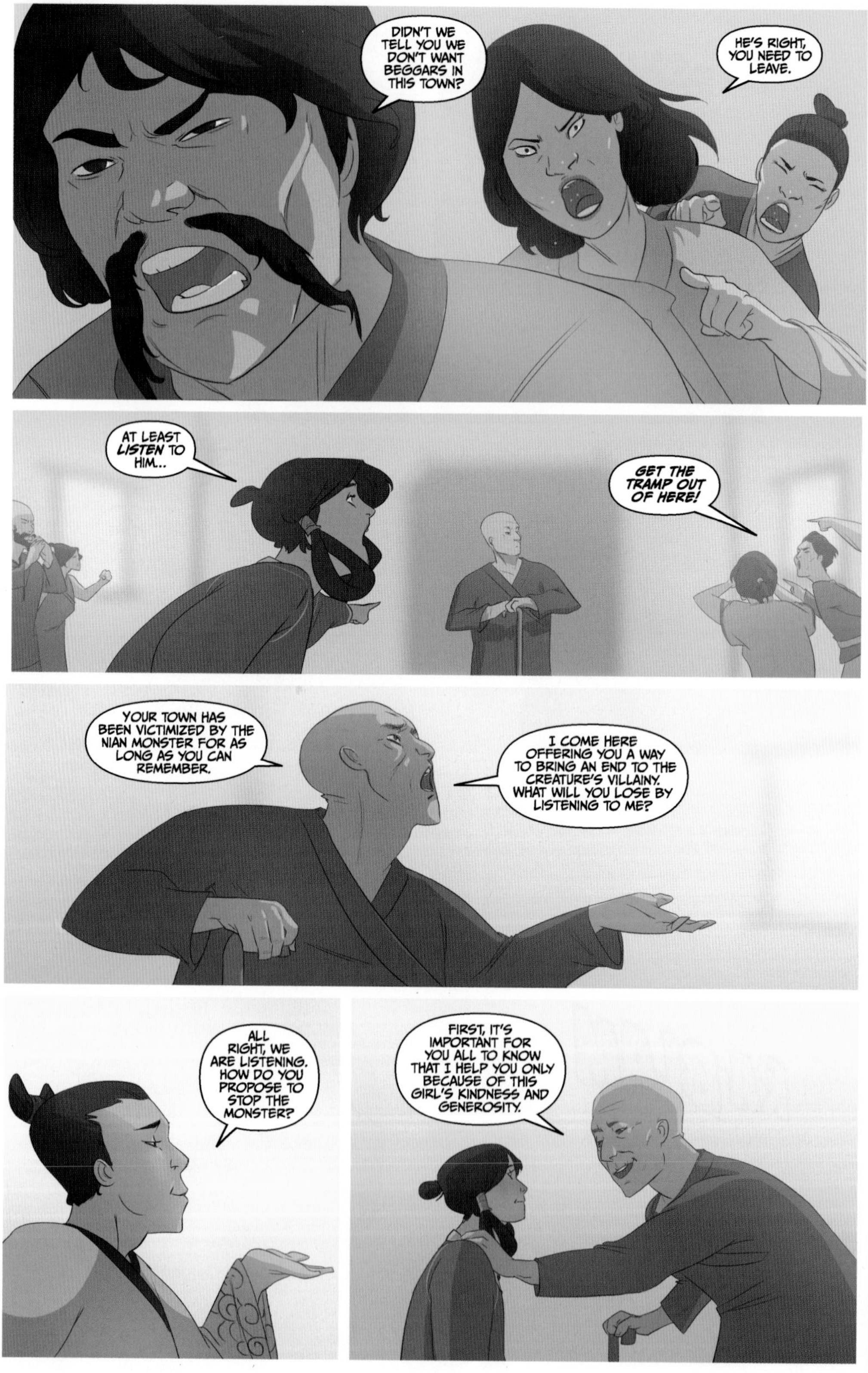
DIDN'T WE TELL YOU WE DON'T WANT BEGGARS IN THIS TOWN?
HE'S RIGHT, YOU NEED TO LEAVE.
AT LEAST *LISTEN* TO HIM...
GET THE TRAMP OUT OF HERE!
YOUR TOWN HAS BEEN VICTIMIZED BY THE NIAN MONSTER FOR AS LONG AS YOU CAN REMEMBER.
I COME HERE OFFERING YOU A WAY TO BRING AN END TO THE CREATURE'S VILLAINY. WHAT WILL YOU LOSE BY LISTENING TO ME?
ALL RIGHT, WE ARE LISTENING. HOW DO YOU PROPOSE TO STOP THE MONSTER?
FIRST, IT'S IMPORTANT FOR YOU ALL TO KNOW THAT I HELP YOU ONLY BECAUSE OF THIS GIRL'S KINDNESS AND GENEROSITY.

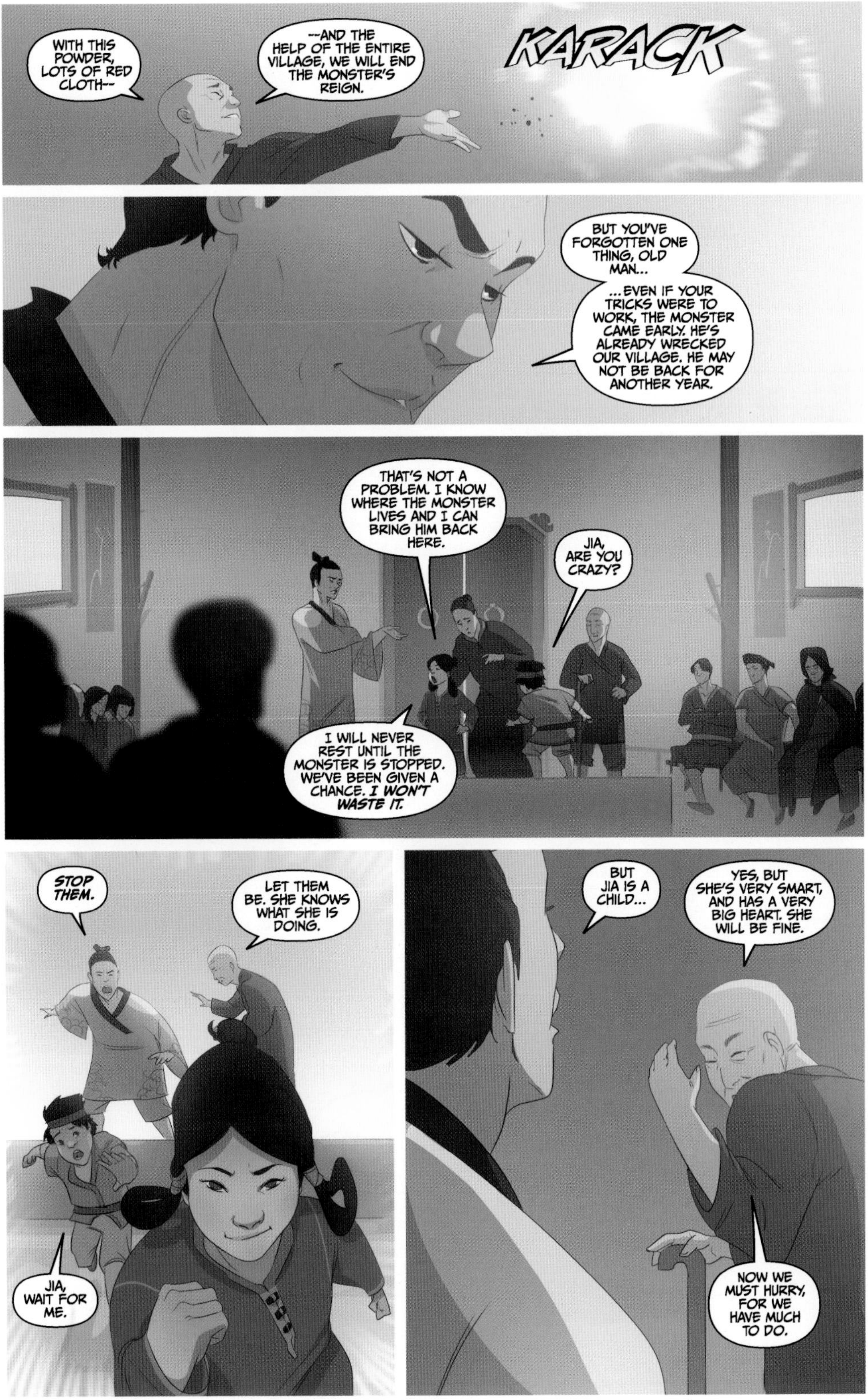
WITH THIS POWDER, LOTS OF RED CLOTH--
--AND THE HELP OF THE ENTIRE VILLAGE, WE WILL END THE MONSTER'S REIGN.
KARACK
BUT YOU'VE FORGOTTEN ONE THING, OLD MAN...
...EVEN IF YOUR TRICKS WERE TO WORK, THE MONSTER CAME EARLY. HE'S ALREADY WRECKED OUR VILLAGE. HE MAY NOT BE BACK FOR ANOTHER YEAR.
THAT'S NOT A PROBLEM. I KNOW WHERE THE MONSTER LIVES AND I CAN BRING HIM BACK HERE.
JIA, ARE YOU CRAZY?
I WILL NEVER REST UNTIL THE MONSTER IS STOPPED. WE'VE BEEN GIVEN A CHANCE. I WON'T WASTE IT.
STOP THEM.
LET THEM BE. SHE KNOWS WHAT SHE IS DOING.
JIA, WAIT FOR ME.
BUT JIA IS A CHILD...
YES, BUT SHE'S VERY SMART, AND HAS A VERY BIG HEART. SHE WILL BE FINE.
NOW WE MUST HURRY, FOR WE HAVE MUCH TO DO.

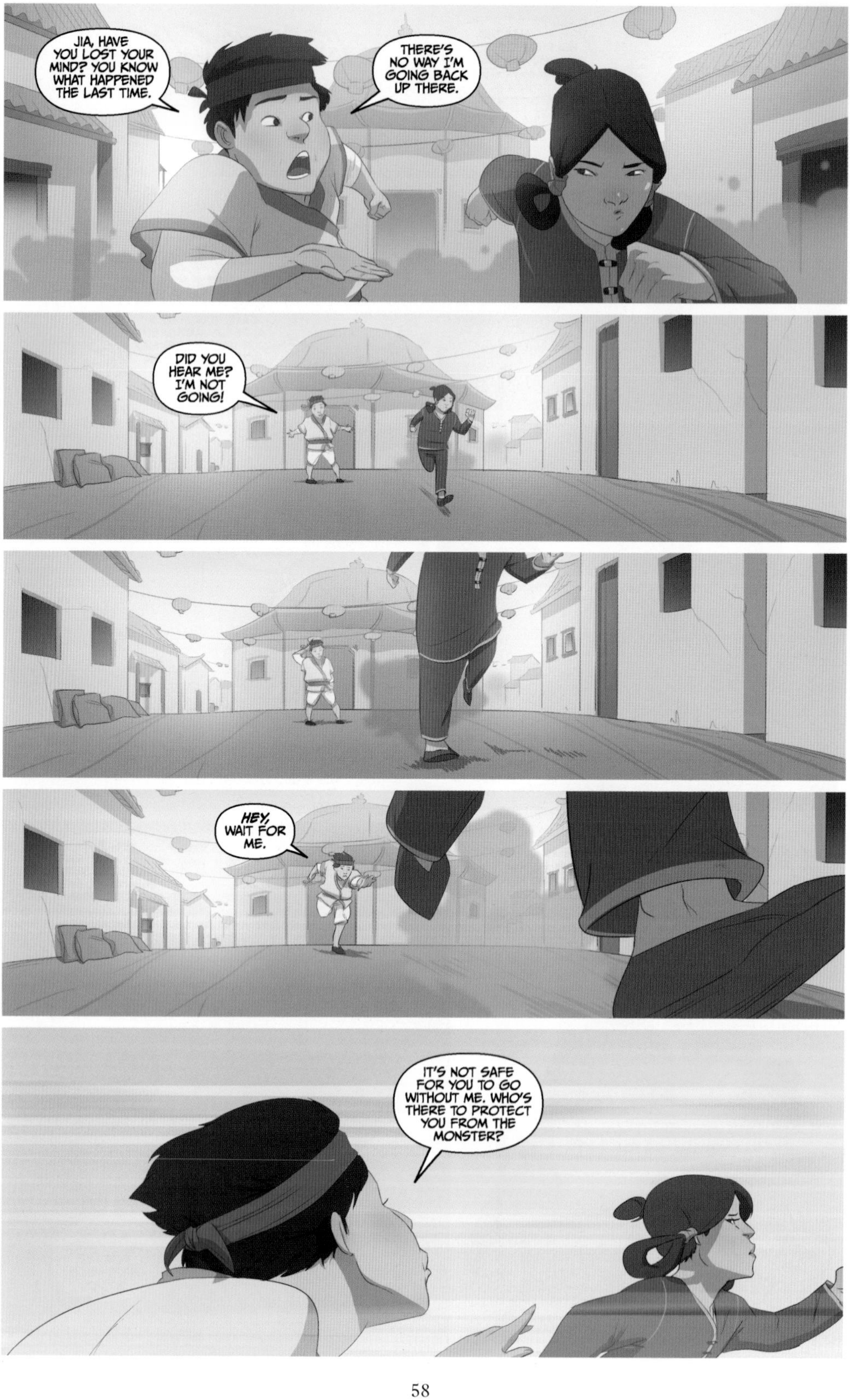
JIA, HAVE YOU LOST YOUR MIND? YOU KNOW WHAT HAPPENED THE LAST TIME.
THERE'S NO WAY I'M GOING BACK UP THERE.
DID YOU HEAR ME? I'M NOT GOING!
HEY, WAIT FOR ME.
IT'S NOT SAFE FOR YOU TO GO WITHOUT ME. WHO'S THERE TO PROTECT YOU FROM THE MONSTER?

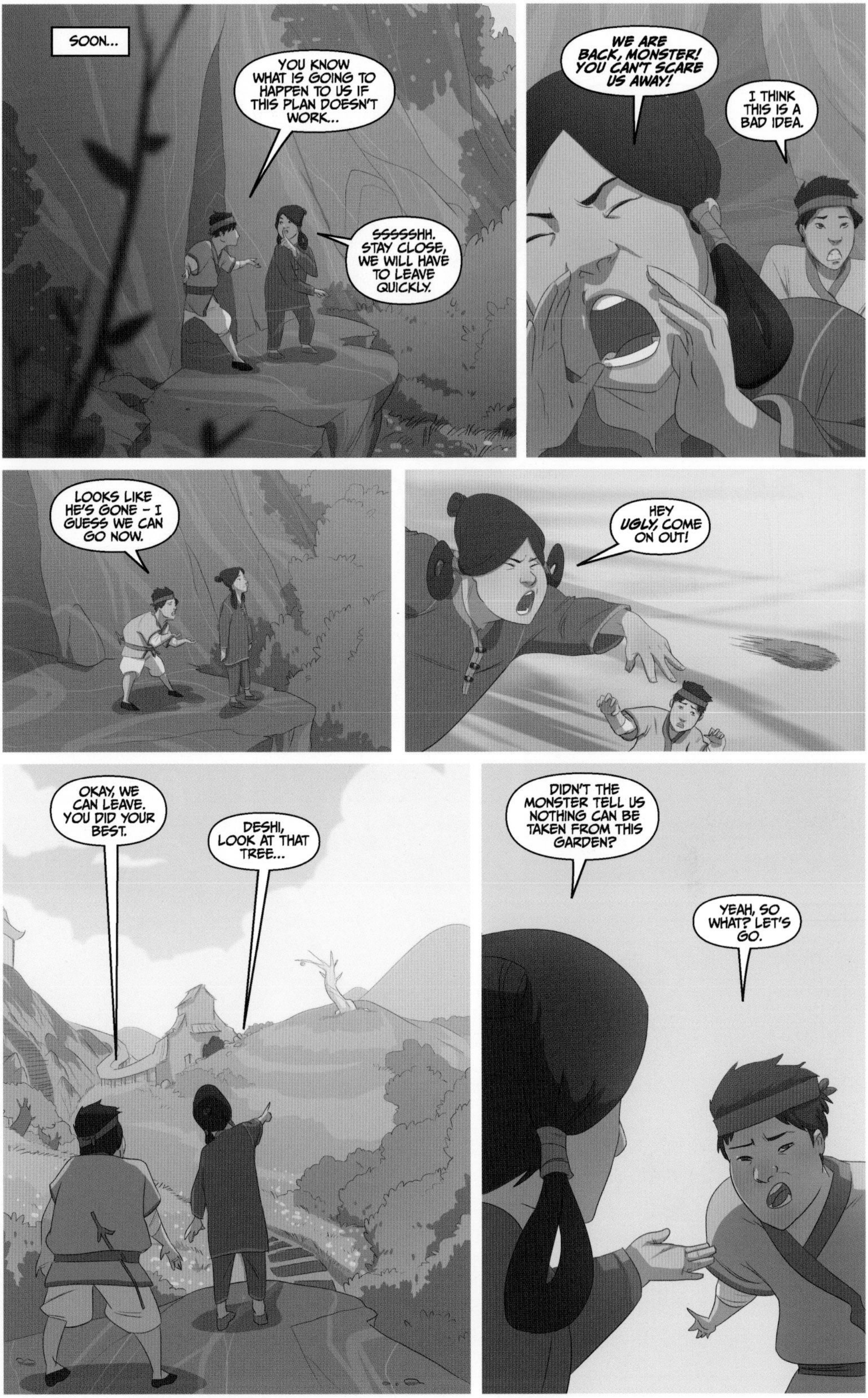
SOON...
YOU KNOW WHAT IS GOING TO HAPPEN TO US IF THIS PLAN DOESN'T WORK...
SSSSSSHH. STAY CLOSE, WE WILL HAVE TO LEAVE QUICKLY.
WE ARE BACK, MONSTER! YOU CAN'T SCARE US AWAY!
I THINK THIS IS A BAD IDEA.
LOOKS LIKE HE'S GONE – I GUESS WE CAN GO NOW.
HEY UGLY, COME ON OUT!
OKAY, WE CAN LEAVE. YOU DID YOUR BEST.
DESHI, LOOK AT THAT TREE...
DIDN'T THE MONSTER TELL US NOTHING CAN BE TAKEN FROM THIS GARDEN?
YEAH, SO WHAT? LET'S GO.

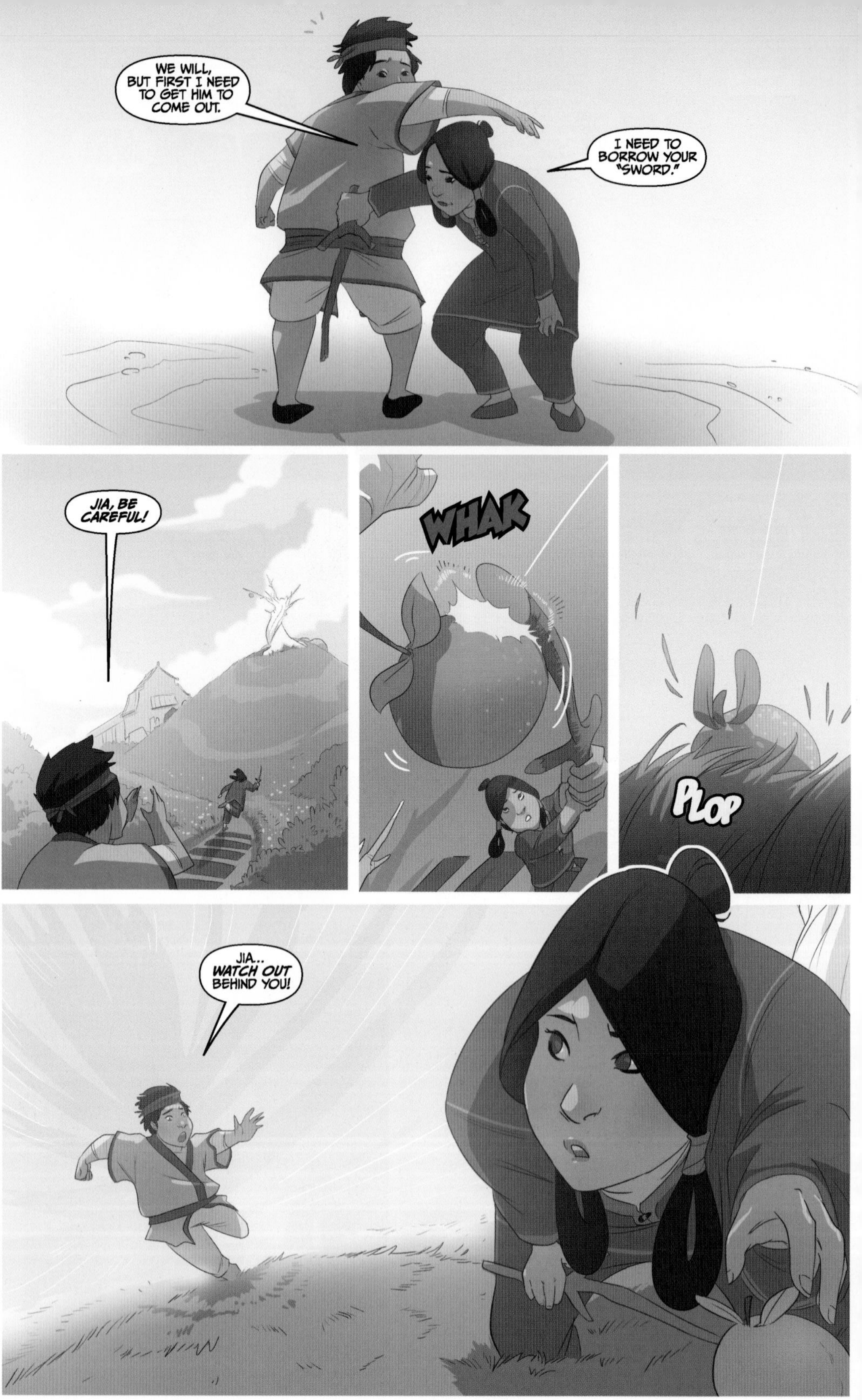
WE WILL, BUT FIRST I NEED TO GET HIM TO COME OUT.
I NEED TO BORROW YOUR "SWORD."
JIA, BE CAREFUL!
WHAK
PLOP
JIA.. WATCH OUT BEHIND YOU!

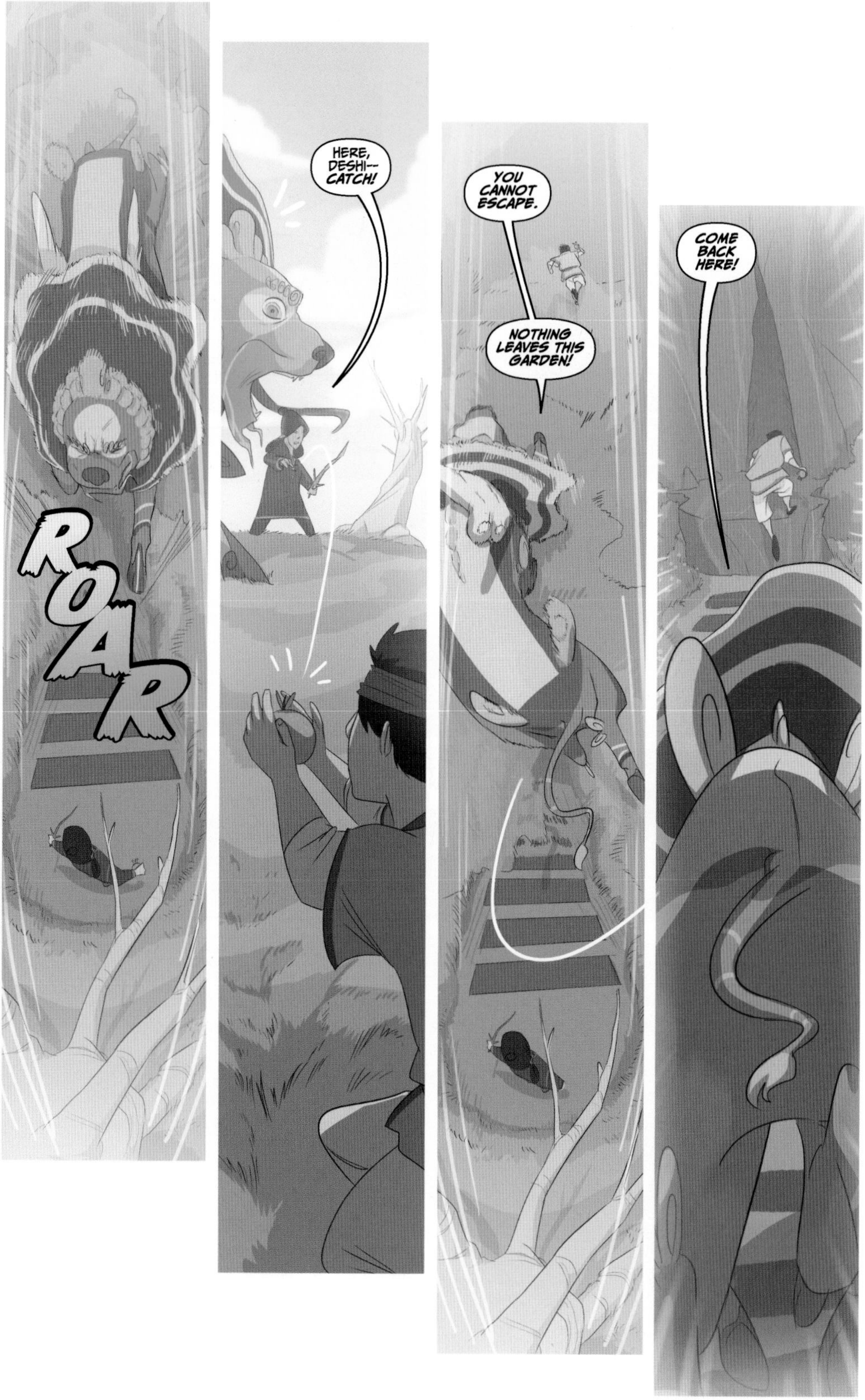
ROAR
HERE, DESHI-- CATCH!
YOU CANNOT ESCAPE.
NOTHING LEAVES THIS GARDEN!
COME BACK HERE!

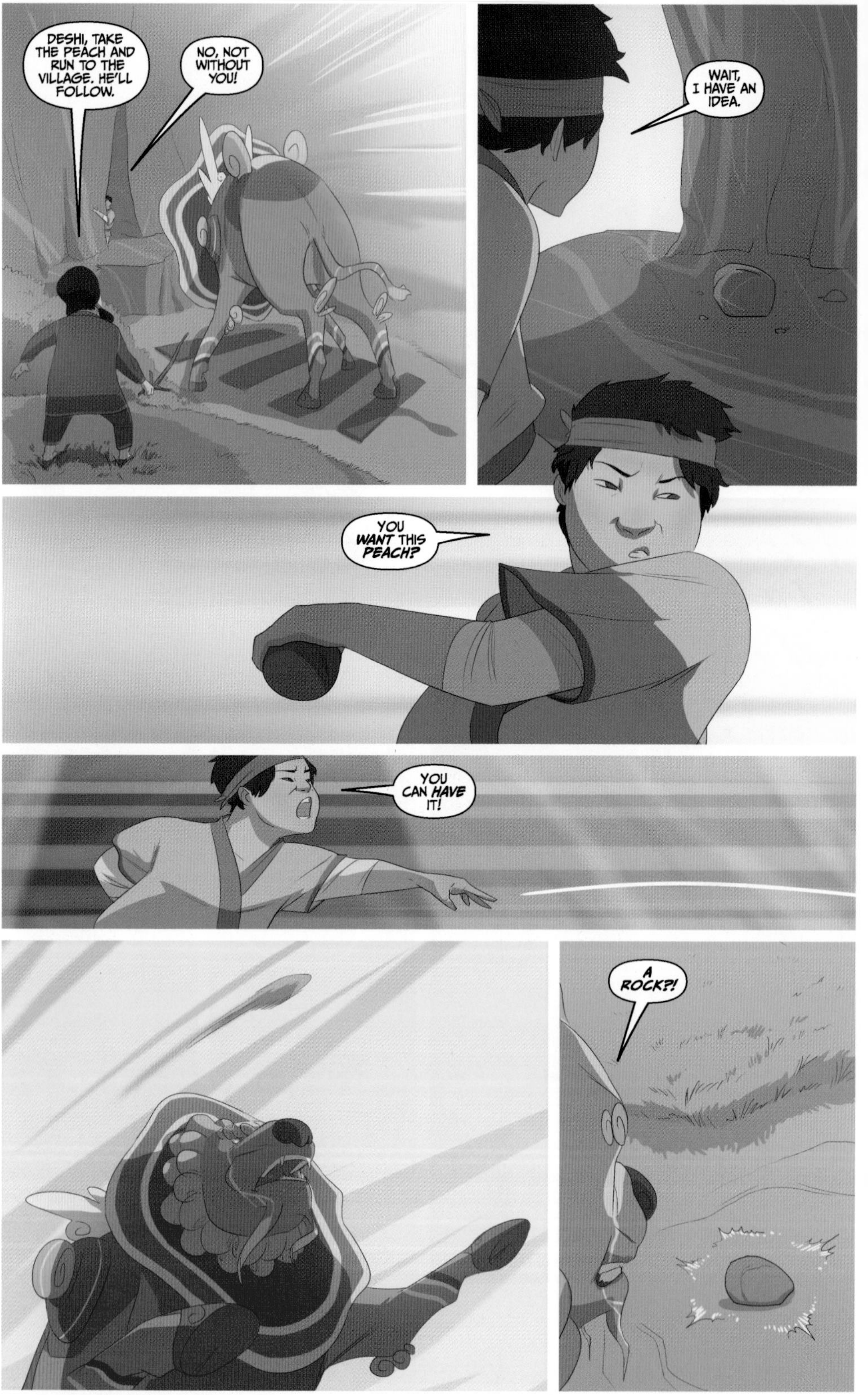
DESHI, TAKE THE PEACH AND RUN TO THE VILLAGE. HE'LL FOLLOW.
NO, NOT WITHOUT YOU!
WAIT, I HAVE AN IDEA.
YOU *WANT* THIS *PEACH?*
YOU CAN *HAVE* IT!
A *ROCK?!*

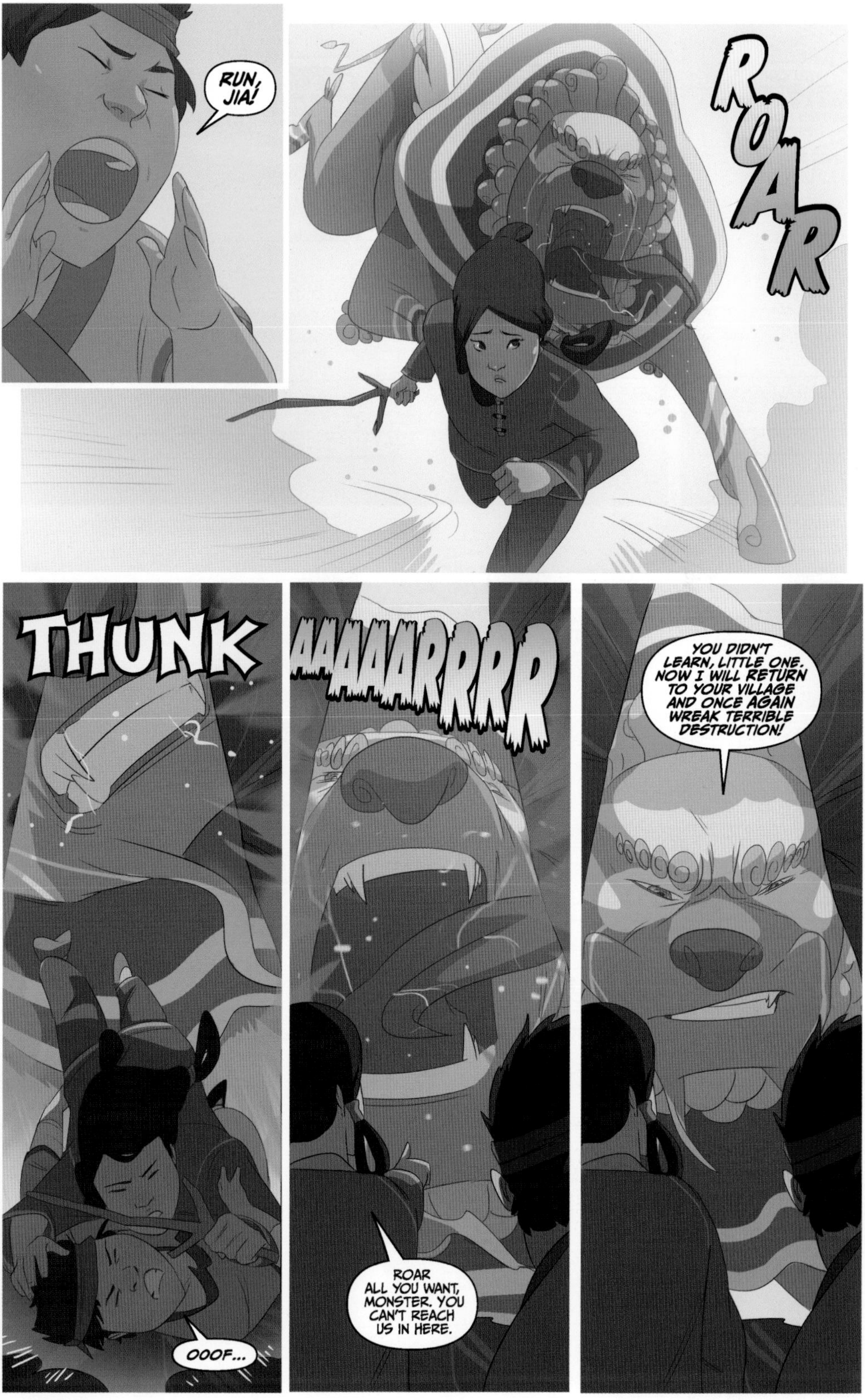
RUN, JIA!
ROAR
THUNK
OOOF...
AAAAARRRR
ROAR ALL YOU WANT, MONSTER. YOU CAN'T REACH US IN HERE.
YOU DIDN'T LEARN, LITTLE ONE. NOW I WILL RETURN TO YOUR VILLAGE AND ONCE AGAIN WREAK TERRIBLE DESTRUCTION!

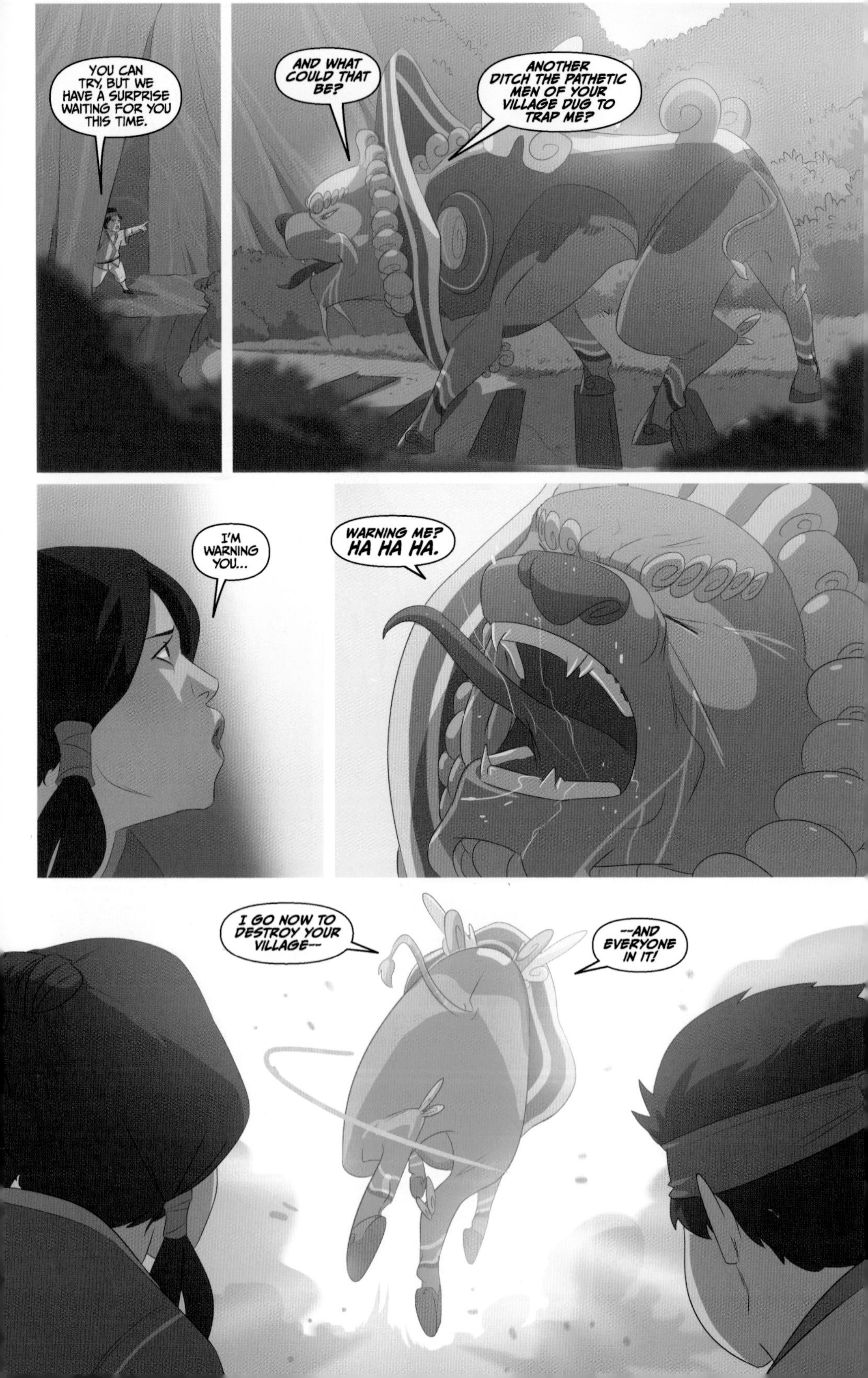

YOU CAN TRY, BUT WE HAVE A SURPRISE WAITING FOR YOU THIS TIME.
AND WHAT COULD THAT BE?
ANOTHER DITCH THE PATHETIC MEN OF YOUR VILLAGE DUG TO TRAP ME?
I'M WARNING YOU...
WARNING ME? HA HA HA.
I GO NOW TO DESTROY YOUR VILLAGE--
--AND EVERYONE IN IT!

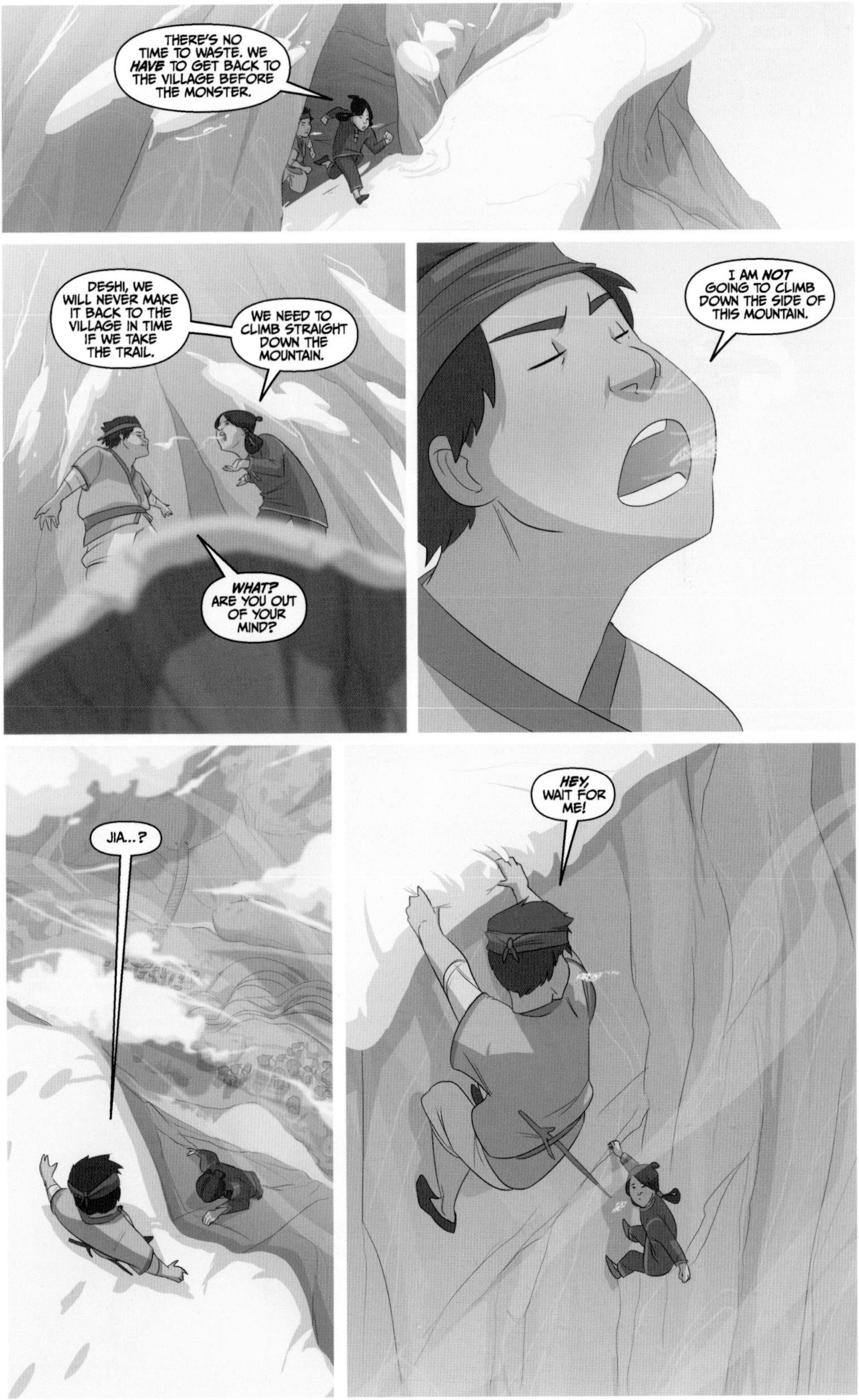
THERE'S NO TIME TO WASTE. WE *HAVE* TO GET BACK TO THE VILLAGE BEFORE THE MONSTER.
DESHI, WE WILL NEVER MAKE IT BACK TO THE VILLAGE IN TIME IF WE TAKE THE TRAIL.
WE NEED TO CLIMB STRAIGHT DOWN THE MOUNTAIN.
WHAT? ARE YOU OUT OF YOUR MIND?
I AM *NOT* GOING TO CLIMB DOWN THE SIDE OF THIS MOUNTAIN.
JIA...?
HEY, WAIT FOR ME!

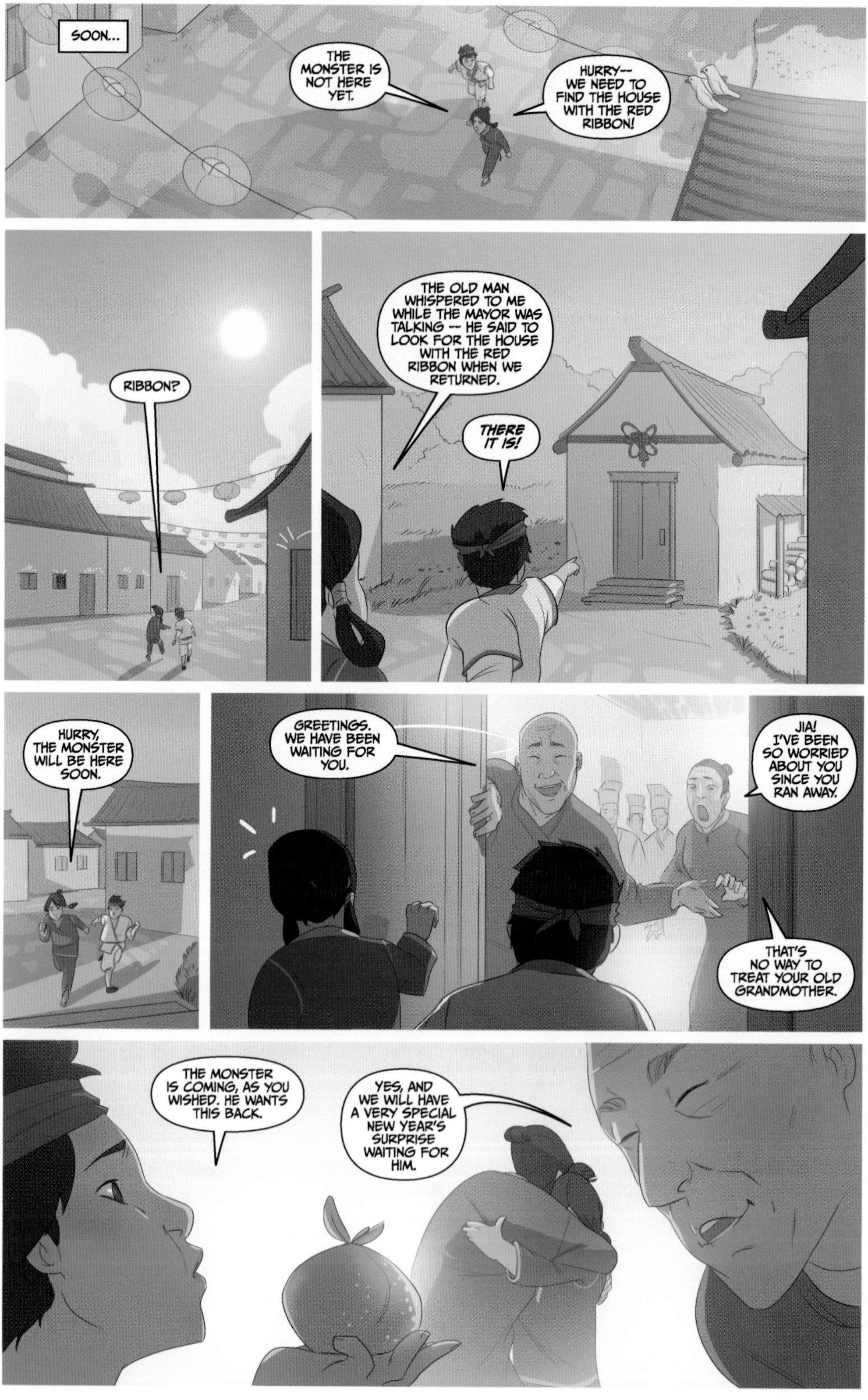
SOON...
THE MONSTER IS NOT HERE YET.
HURRY-- WE NEED TO FIND THE HOUSE WITH THE RED RIBBON!
RIBBON?
THE OLD MAN WHISPERED TO ME WHILE THE MAYOR WAS TALKING -- HE SAID TO LOOK FOR THE HOUSE WITH THE RED RIBBON WHEN WE RETURNED.
THERE IT IS!
HURRY, THE MONSTER WILL BE HERE SOON.
GREETINGS. WE HAVE BEEN WAITING FOR YOU.
JIA! I'VE BEEN SO WORRIED ABOUT YOU SINCE YOU RAN AWAY.
THAT'S NO WAY TO TREAT YOUR OLD GRANDMOTHER.
THE MONSTER IS COMING, AS YOU WISHED. HE WANTS THIS BACK.
YES, AND WE WILL HAVE A VERY SPECIAL NEW YEAR'S SURPRISE WAITING FOR HIM.

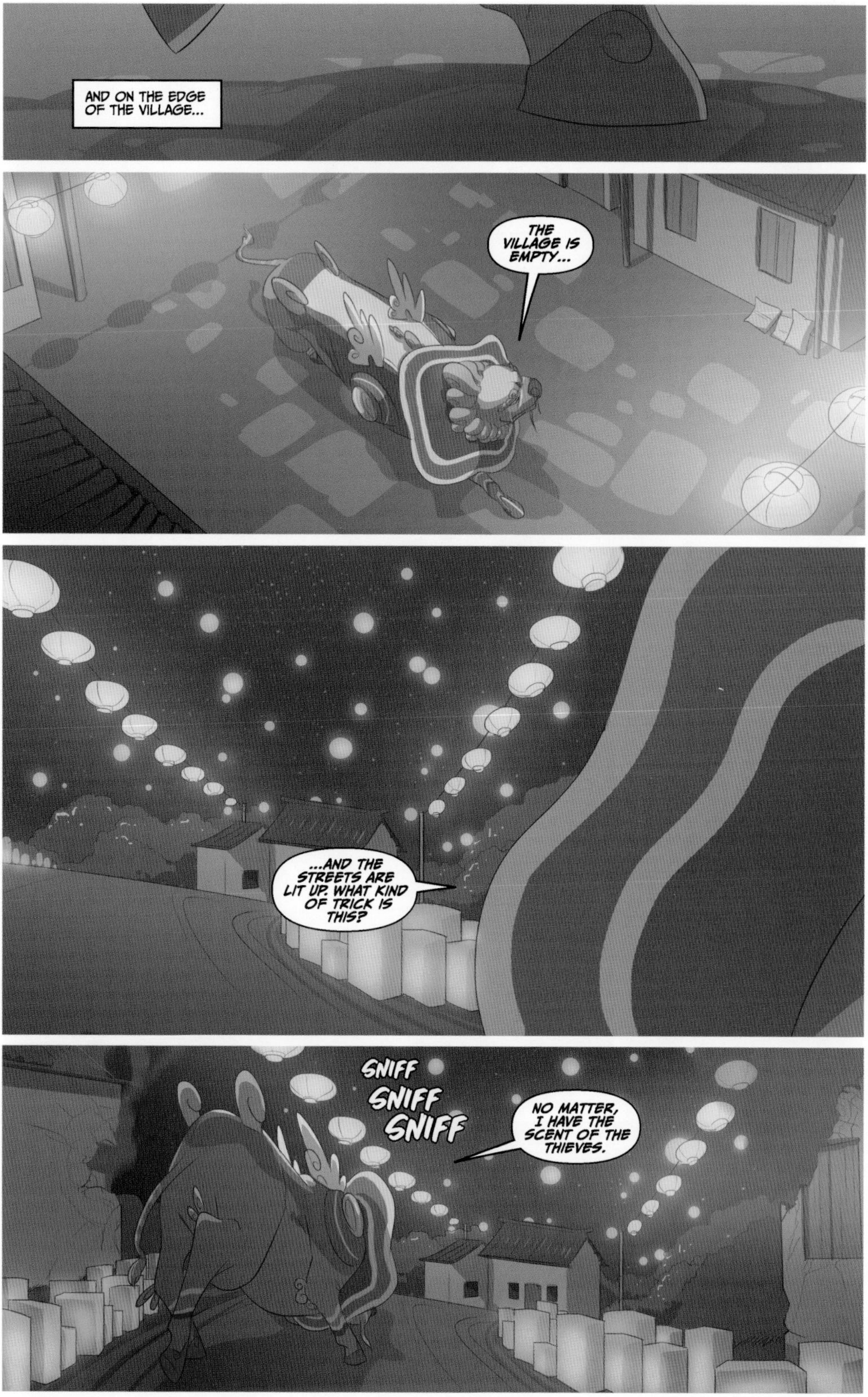
AND ON THE EDGE OF THE VILLAGE...
THE VILLAGE IS EMPTY...
...AND THE STREETS ARE LIT UP. WHAT KIND OF TRICK IS THIS?
SNIFF SNIFF SNIFF
NO MATTER, I HAVE THE SCENT OF THE THIEVES.

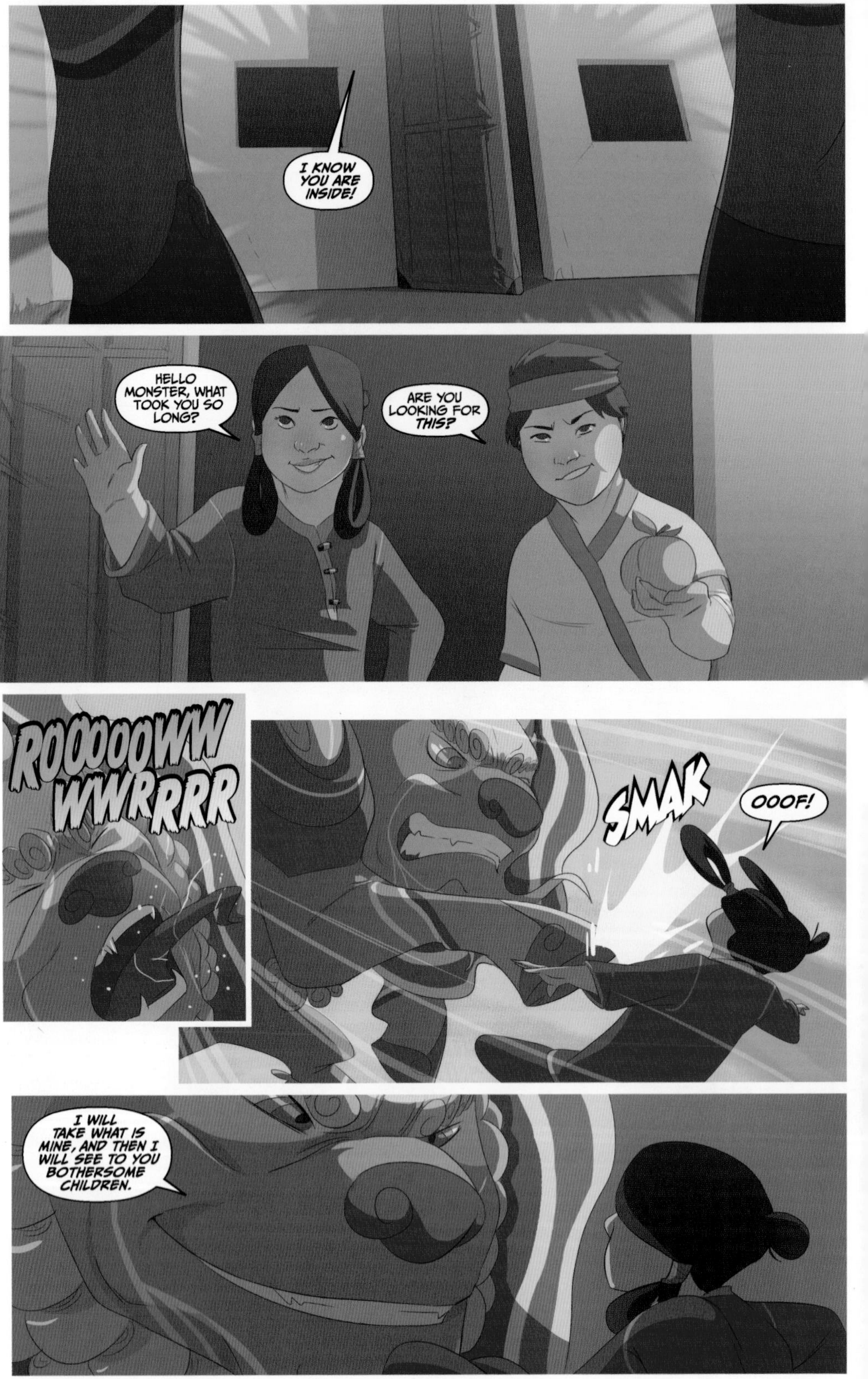

I KNOW YOU ARE INSIDE!
HELLO MONSTER, WHAT TOOK YOU SO LONG?
ARE YOU LOOKING FOR THIS?
ROOOOOWW WWRRRR
SMAK
OOOF!
I WILL TAKE WHAT IS MINE, AND THEN I WILL SEE TO YOU BOTHERSOME CHILDREN.

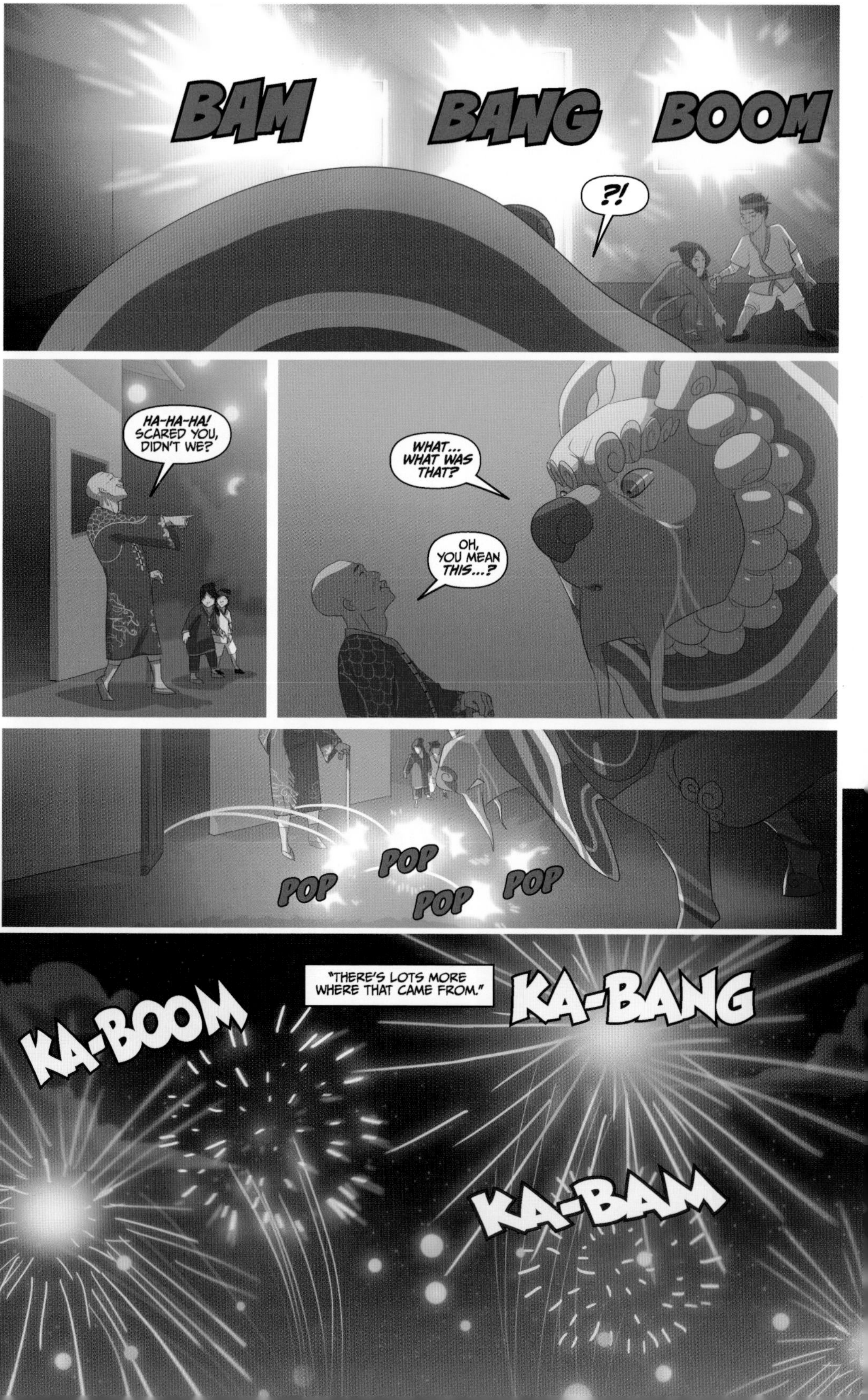
BAM
BANG
BOOM
?!
HA-HA-HA! SCARED YOU, DIDN'T WE?
WHAT... WHAT WAS THAT?
OH, YOU MEAN THIS...?
POP
POP
POP
POP
"THERE'S LOTS MORE WHERE THAT CAME FROM."
KA-BOOM
KA-BANG
KA-BAM

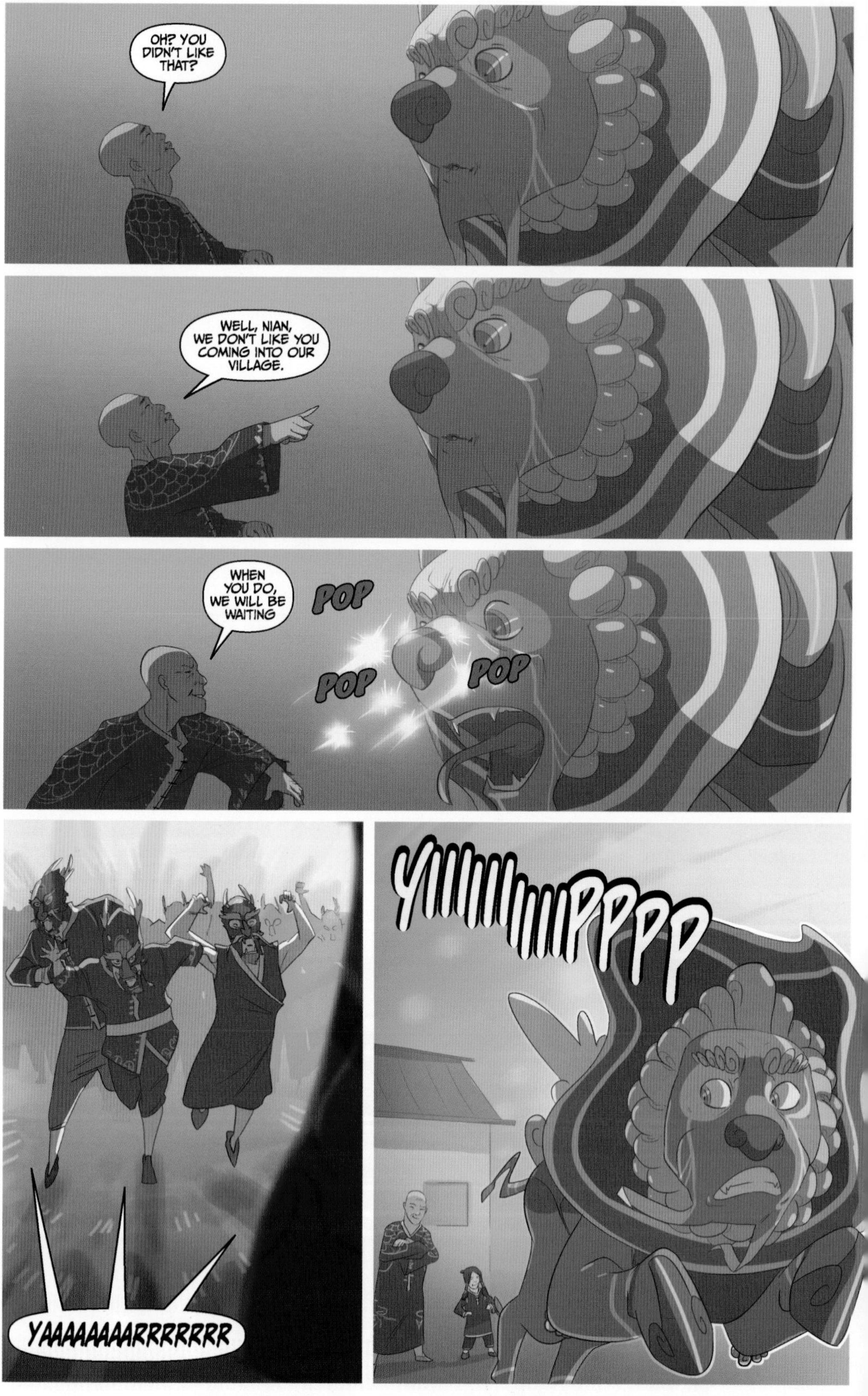
OH? YOU DIDN'T LIKE THAT?
WELL, NIAN, WE DON'T LIKE YOU COMING INTO OUR VILLAGE.
WHEN YOU DO, WE WILL BE WAITING
POP
POP
POP
YAAAAAAAARRRRRRR
YIIIIIIIIPPPP

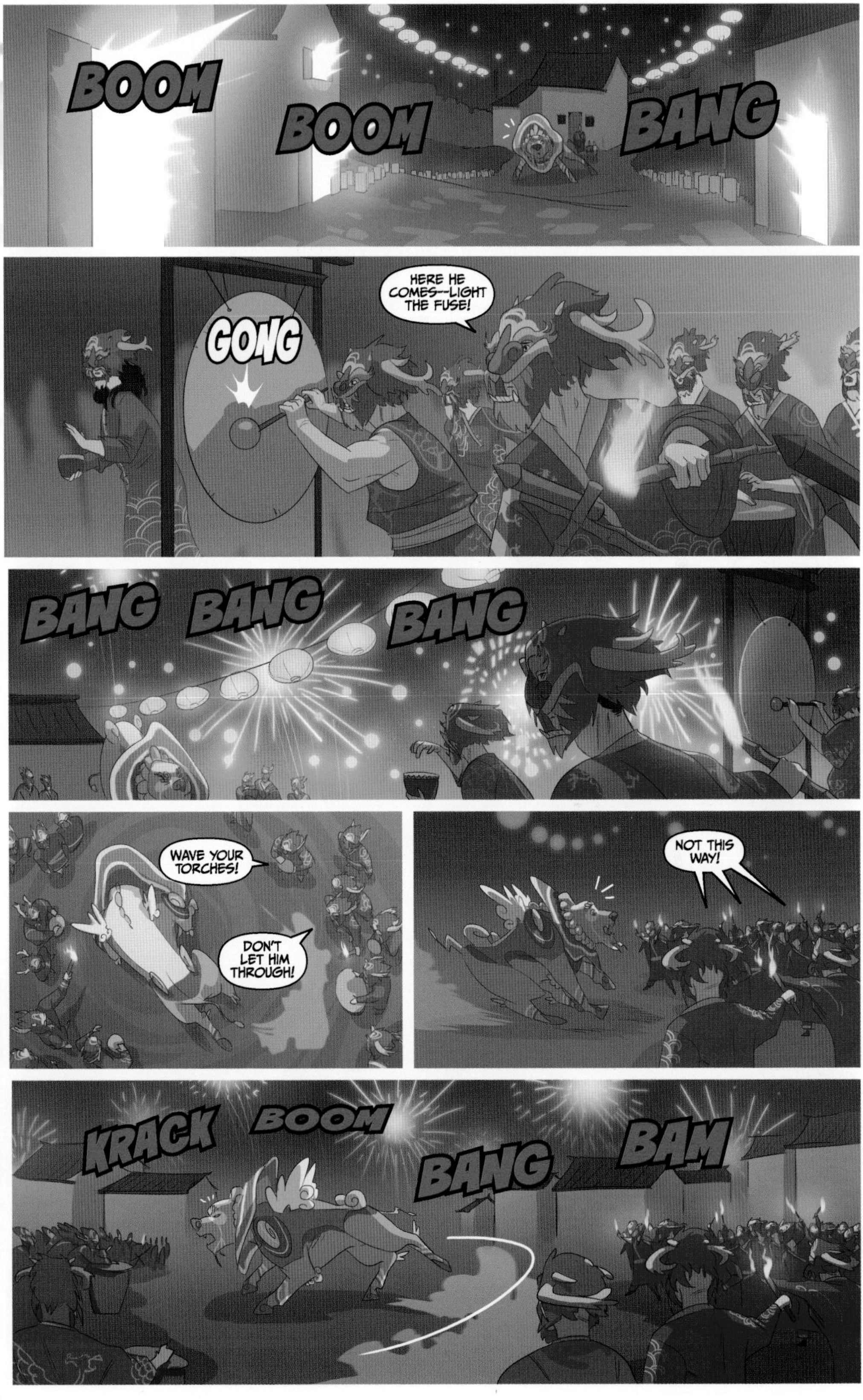
BOOM
BOOM
BANG
GONG
HERE HE COMES--LIGHT THE FUSE!
BANG
BANG
BANG
WAVE YOUR TORCHES!
DON'T LET HIM THROUGH!
NOT THIS WAY!
KRACK
BOOM
BANG
BAM

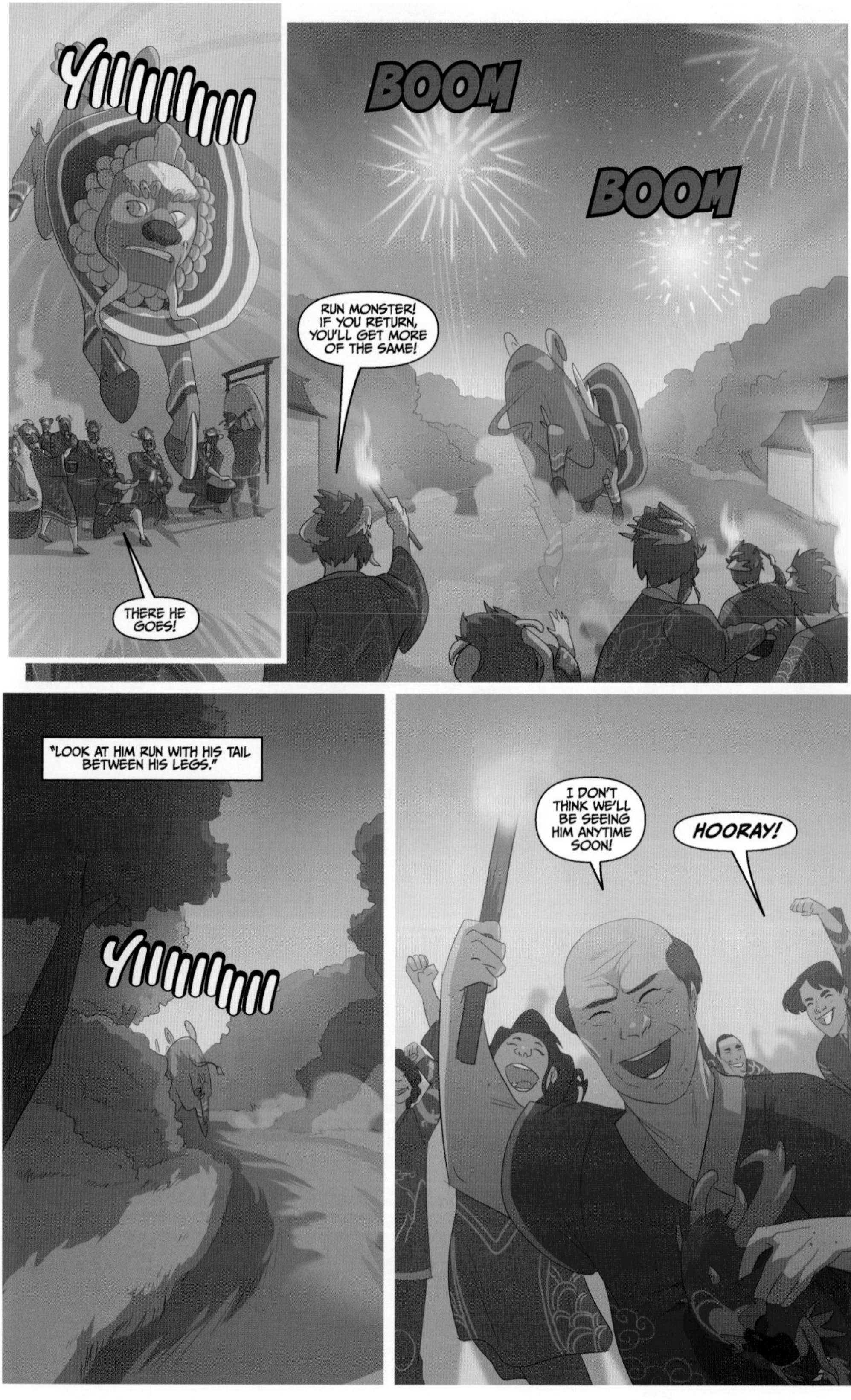
YIIIIIIIII
THERE HE GOES!
BOOM
BOOM
RUN MONSTER! IF YOU RETURN, YOU'LL GET MORE OF THE SAME!
"LOOK AT HIM RUN WITH HIS TAIL BETWEEN HIS LEGS."
YIIIIIIIII
I DON'T THINK WE'LL BE SEEING HIM ANYTIME SOON!
HOORAY!

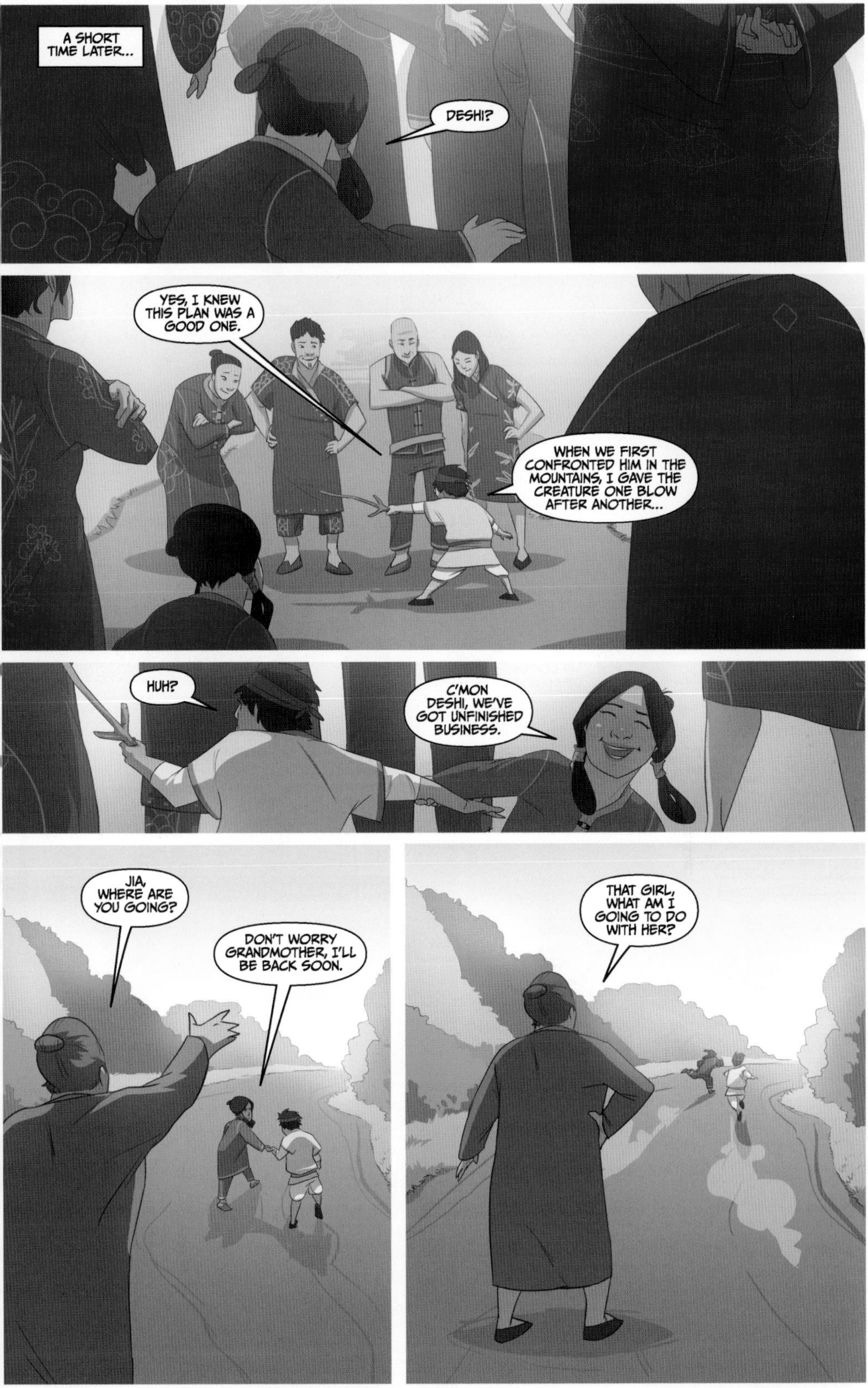
A SHORT TIME LATER...
DESHI?
YES, I KNEW THIS PLAN WAS A GOOD ONE.
WHEN WE FIRST CONFRONTED HIM IN THE MOUNTAINS, I GAVE THE CREATURE ONE BLOW AFTER ANOTHER...
HUH?
C'MON DESHI, WE'VE GOT UNFINISHED BUSINESS.
JIA, WHERE ARE YOU GOING?
DON'T WORRY GRANDMOTHER, I'LL BE BACK SOON.
THAT GIRL, WHAT AM I GOING TO DO WITH HER?

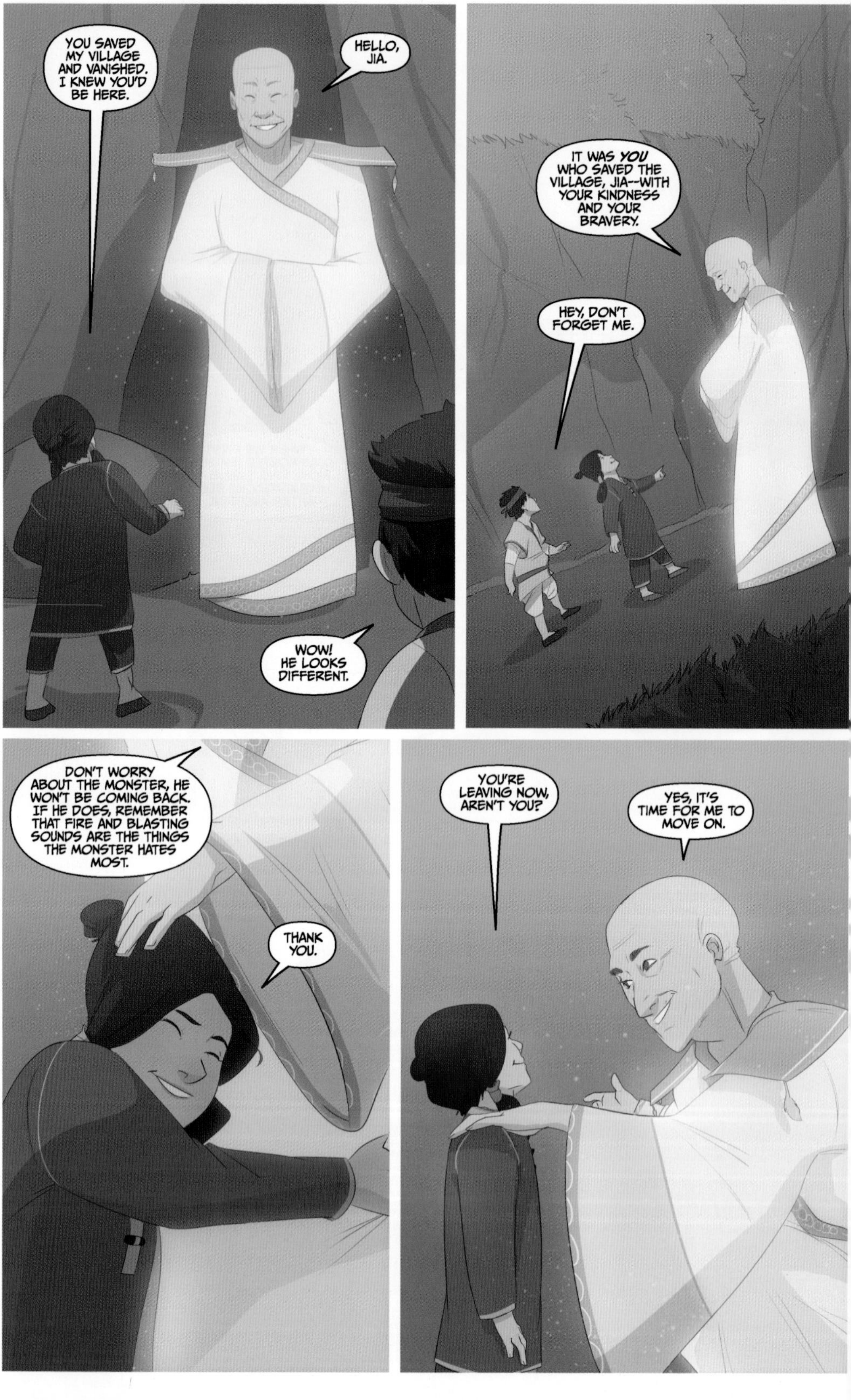
YOU SAVED MY VILLAGE AND VANISHED. I KNEW YOU'D BE HERE.
HELLO, JIA.
WOW! HE LOOKS DIFFERENT.
IT WAS *YOU* WHO SAVED THE VILLAGE, JIA--WITH YOUR KINDNESS AND YOUR BRAVERY.
HEY, DON'T FORGET ME.
DON'T WORRY ABOUT THE MONSTER, HE WON'T BE COMING BACK. IF HE DOES, REMEMBER THAT FIRE AND BLASTING SOUNDS ARE THE THINGS THE MONSTER HATES MOST.
THANK YOU.
YOU'RE LEAVING NOW, AREN'T YOU?
YES, IT'S TIME FOR ME TO MOVE ON.

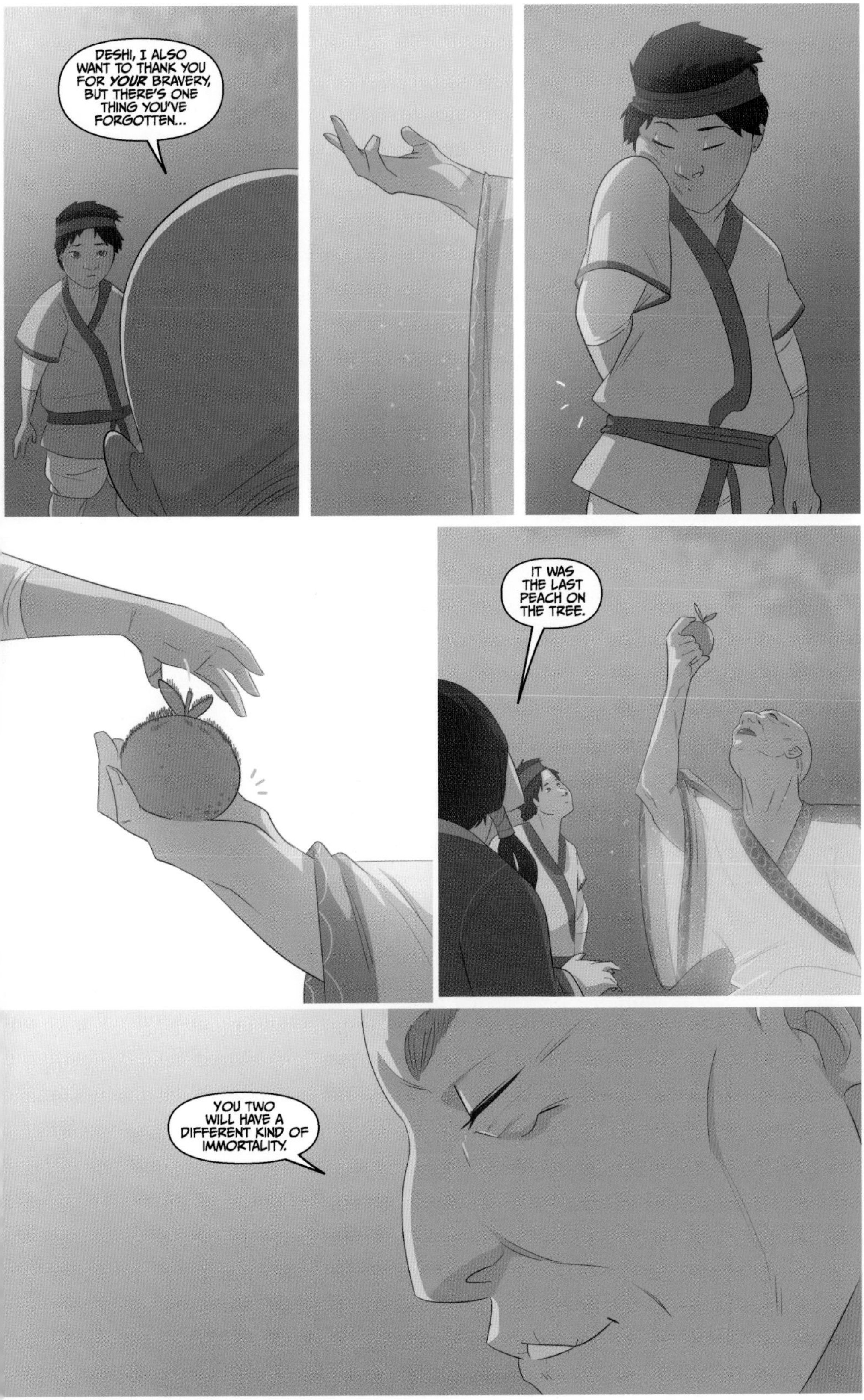
DESHI, I ALSO WANT TO THANK YOU FOR *YOUR* BRAVERY, BUT THERE'S ONE THING YOU'VE FORGOTTEN...
IT WAS THE LAST PEACH ON THE TREE.
YOU TWO WILL HAVE A DIFFERENT KIND OF IMMORTALITY.

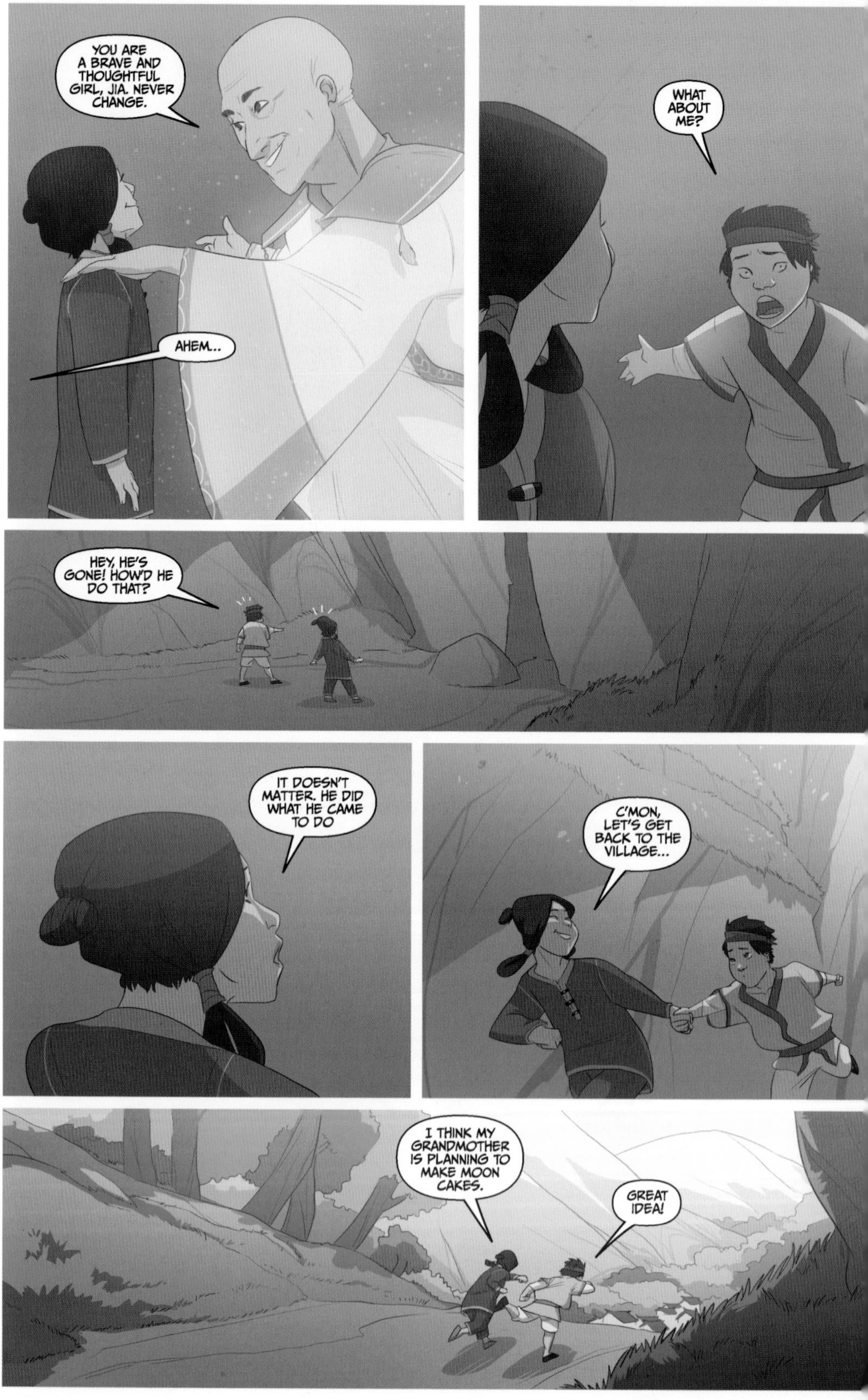
YOU ARE A BRAVE AND THOUGHTFUL GIRL, JIA. NEVER CHANGE.
AHEM...
WHAT ABOUT ME?
HEY, HE'S GONE! HOW'D HE DO THAT?
IT DOESN'T MATTER. HE DID WHAT HE CAME TO DO
C'MON, LET'S GET BACK TO THE VILLAGE...
I THINK MY GRANDMOTHER IS PLANNING TO MAKE MOON CAKES.
GREAT IDEA!

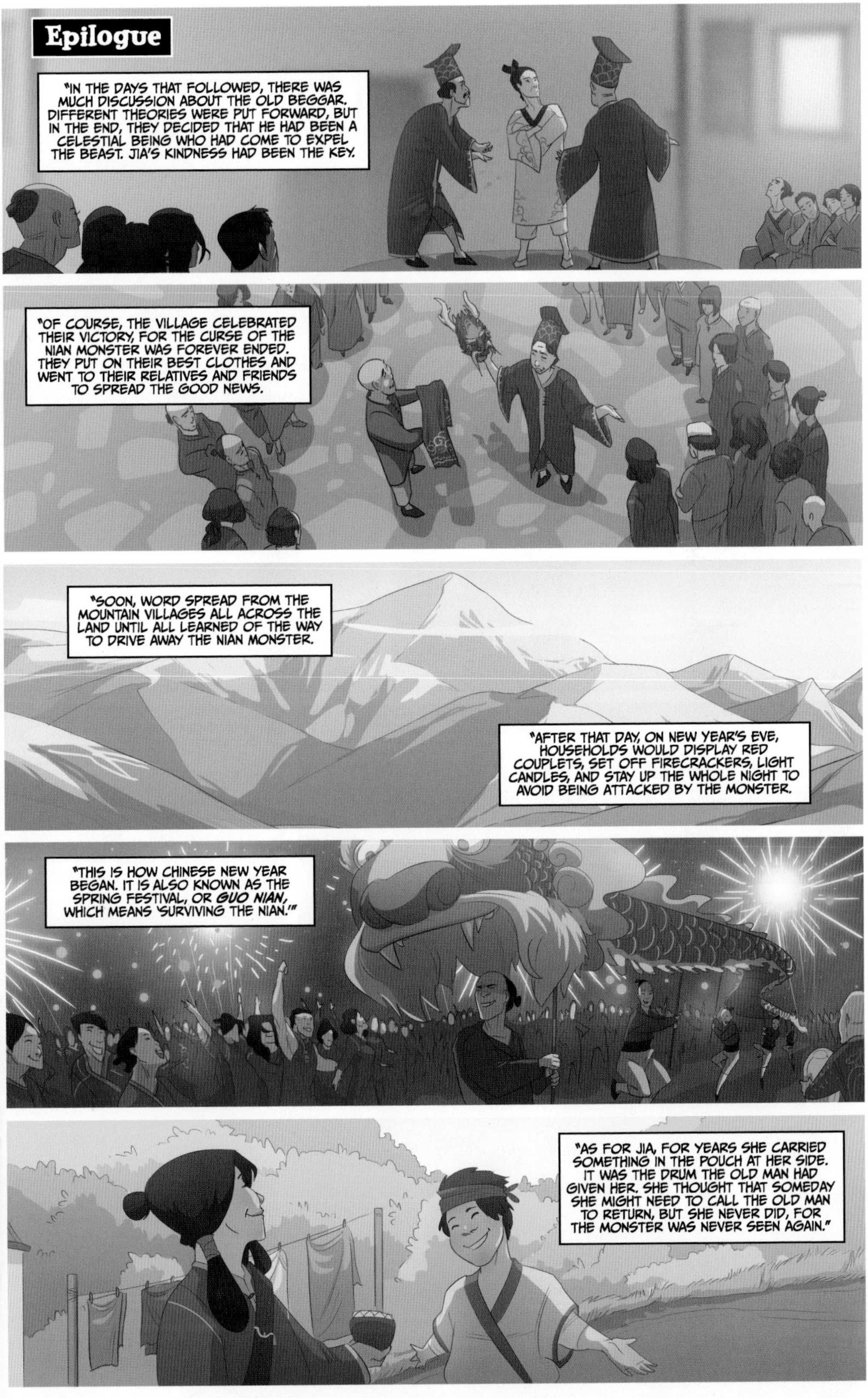
Epilogue
"IN THE DAYS THAT FOLLOWED, THERE WAS MUCH DISCUSSION ABOUT THE OLD BEGGAR. DIFFERENT THEORIES WERE PUT FORWARD, BUT IN THE END, THEY DECIDED THAT HE HAD BEEN A CELESTIAL BEING WHO HAD COME TO EXPEL THE BEAST. JIA'S KINDNESS HAD BEEN THE KEY.
"OF COURSE, THE VILLAGE CELEBRATED THEIR VICTORY, FOR THE CURSE OF THE NIAN MONSTER WAS FOREVER ENDED. THEY PUT ON THEIR BEST CLOTHES AND WENT TO THEIR RELATIVES AND FRIENDS TO SPREAD THE GOOD NEWS.
"SOON, WORD SPREAD FROM THE MOUNTAIN VILLAGES ALL ACROSS THE LAND UNTIL ALL LEARNED OF THE WAY TO DRIVE AWAY THE NIAN MONSTER.
"AFTER THAT DAY, ON NEW YEAR'S EVE, HOUSEHOLDS WOULD DISPLAY RED COUPLETS, SET OFF FIRECRACKERS, LIGHT CANDLES, AND STAY UP THE WHOLE NIGHT TO AVOID BEING ATTACKED BY THE MONSTER.
"THIS IS HOW CHINESE NEW YEAR BEGAN. IT IS ALSO KNOWN AS THE SPRING FESTIVAL, OR *GUO NIAN*, WHICH MEANS 'SURVIVING THE NIAN.'"
"AS FOR JIA, FOR YEARS SHE CARRIED SOMETHING IN THE POUCH AT HER SIDE. IT WAS THE DRUM THE OLD MAN HAD GIVEN HER. SHE THOUGHT THAT SOMEDAY SHE MIGHT NEED TO CALL THE OLD MAN TO RETURN, BUT SHE NEVER DID, FOR THE MONSTER WAS NEVER SEEN AGAIN."

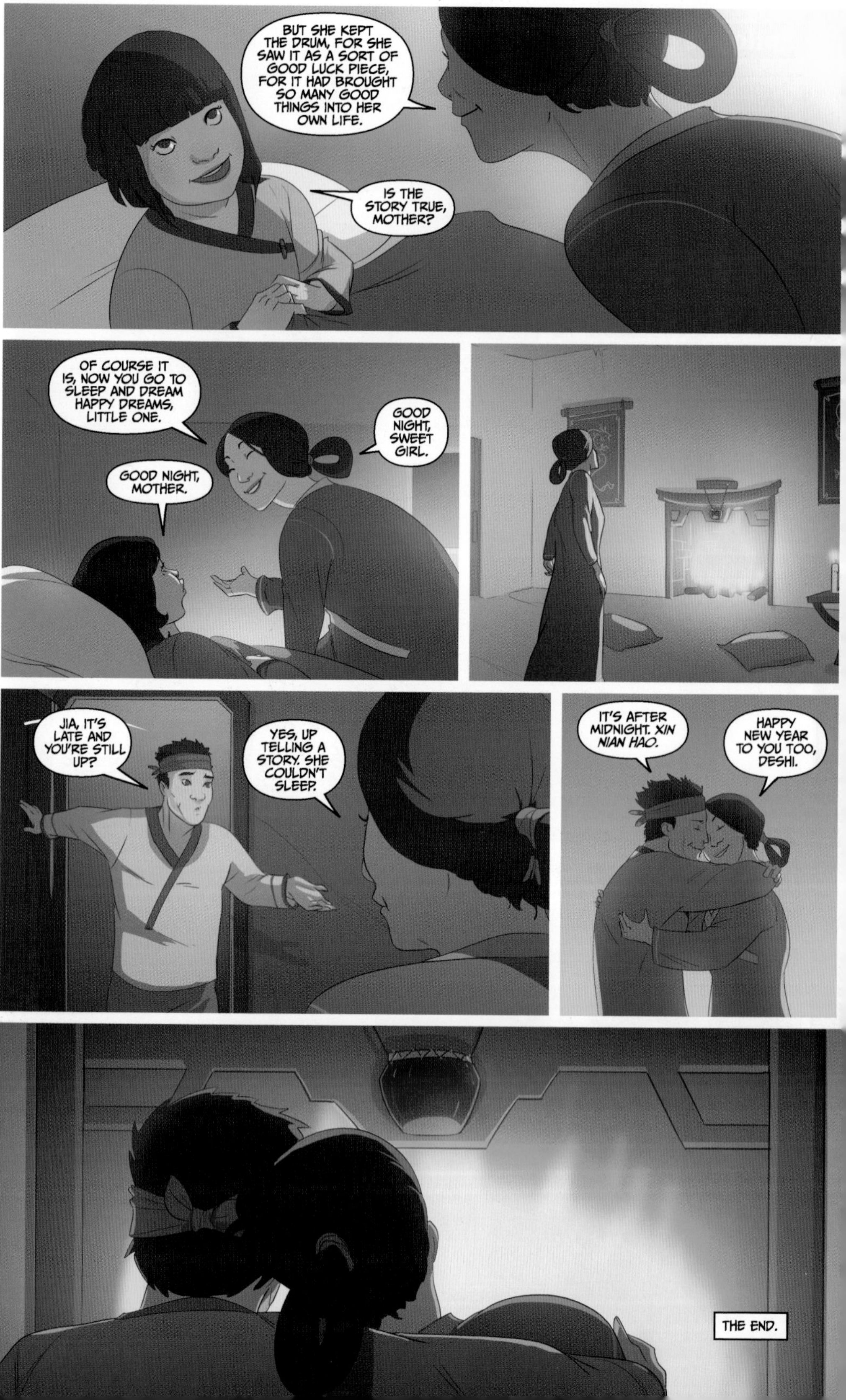
BUT SHE KEPT THE DRUM, FOR SHE SAW IT AS A SORT OF GOOD LUCK PIECE, FOR IT HAD BROUGHT SO MANY GOOD THINGS INTO HER OWN LIFE.
IS THE STORY TRUE, MOTHER?
OF COURSE IT IS, NOW YOU GO TO SLEEP AND DREAM HAPPY DREAMS, LITTLE ONE.
GOOD NIGHT, MOTHER.
GOOD NIGHT, SWEET GIRL.
JIA, IT'S LATE AND YOU'RE STILL UP?
YES, UP TELLING A STORY. SHE COULDN'T SLEEP.
IT'S AFTER MIDNIGHT. XIN NIAN HAO.
HAPPY NEW YEAR TO YOU TOO, DESHI.
THE END.

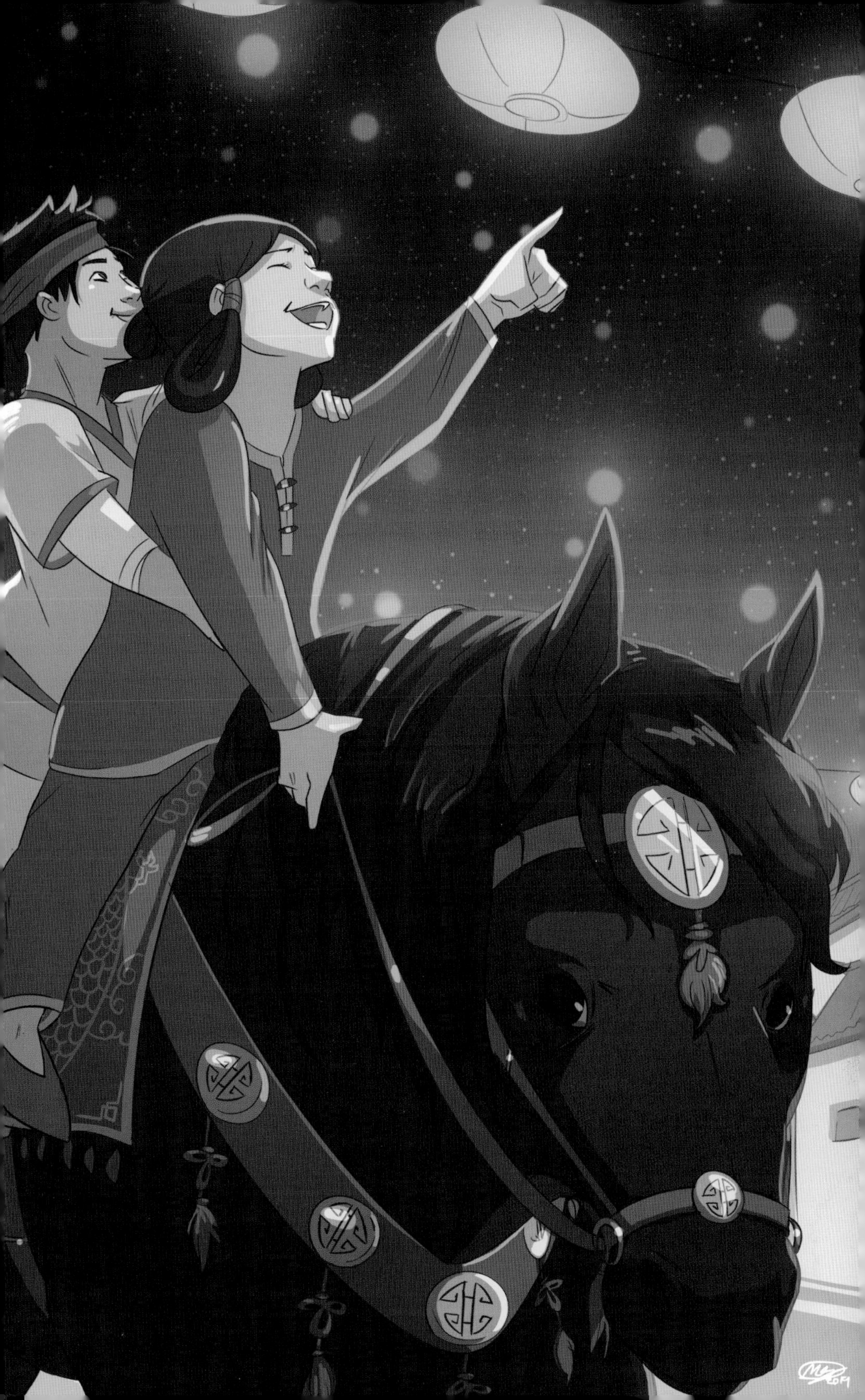

OTHER BOOKS BY ROD ESPINOSA

THE
COURAGEOUS
PRINCESS
BEYOND THE HUNDRED KINGDOMS
ROD ESPINOSA

THE
COURAGEOUS
PRINCESS
THE UNREMEMBERED LANDS
ROD ESPINOSA

THE
COURAGEOUS
PRINCESS
THE DRAGON QUEEN
ROD ESPINOSA

THIS PRINCESS WILL RESCUE HERSELF, THANK YOU VERY MUCH!

The complete trilogy in paperback for the first time!

Available now!
THE COURAGEOUS PRINCESS
VOLUME 1: BEYOND THE HUNDRED KINGDOMS

Once upon a time, a greedy dragon kidnapped a beloved princess . . . but if you think she just waited around for some charming price to rescue her, then you're in for a surprise! Princess Mabelrose may not be the fairest of the land, but she has enough brains and bravery to fend for herself in a fantasy world of danger and adventure!

ISBN 978-1-50671-446-2 / $14.99

THE COURAGEOUS PRINCESS
VOLUME 2: THE UNREMEMBERED LANDS

On her journey home, Princess Mabelrose makes new friends and encounters witches, giants, and another dragon!

ISBN 978-1-50671-447-9 / $14.99

Coming in August, 2020!
THE COURAGEOUS PRINCESS
VOLUME 3: THE DRAGON QUEEN

Mabelrose, her friends, and her father are all captured by the Dragon Queen!

ISBN 978-1-50671-448-6 / $14.99

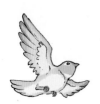

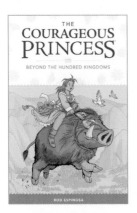

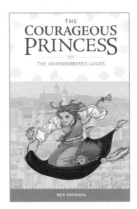

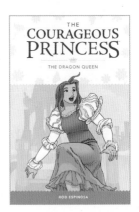

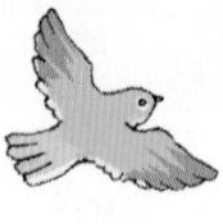